The Illusionist Takes a Holiday

SOLOMON KNIGHT

190 Ann Street, Suite 603
Belleville, Ontario K8N 5G2
CANADA
SolomonKnight.Paladin@gmail.com

ISBN-13:9781724284266
ISBN-10:1724284266

DEDICATION

For all those that put their lives on the line for others.

CONTENTS

BOOKS IN THE SERIES

Evil Lurks in the Dark

The Shadow Man

The Illusionist Takes a Holiday

PREFACE

Due to the story setting, I have used English and Scottish spellings and terms that might be unfamiliar. I have tried to insert interpretations where I felt necessary and hope I have not been bothersome.

This is a work of fiction and all characters are fictional creations. Any resemblance to any real person, living or dead, is entirely coincidental. Although some places or businesses may bear some resemblance to real-life places or businesses, that is also coincidental.

1 A GOOD SAMARITAN

The air was fresh and clean, the sky pale blue with a carefree, feathery cloud drifting aimlessly here and there. A gentle breeze playfully pushed bits of paper around on the street. People jostled to and fro as they went about their business. He took pleasure in the sights, smells and sounds of London.

Born in Edinburgh, Scotland, to parents employed as career diplomats he had lived in various corners of the world. He quite literally received an international education and many fast friendships and tight bonds had been forged that would turn out to be of vital importance to him. He spoke English, German and Cantonese fluently and was passable in Russian by the time he was eighteen years of age.

He had also been an observer of the aftermath of the most contemptible of all violence, that of spousal and child abuse. His introduction to such violence and hopelessness of the victim was a profound epiphany.

It was in his eighteenth year that he was to learn the cruelty of life. While walking in a park, not far from his family's home in Edinburgh, he had observed a young tawny haired beauty, no more than twenty-two years old, sitting on a park bench alone and sobbing as if her heart would break. Not wishing to intrude he had quietly taken a seat on the end of her bench and waited in silence for what he did not know. It wasn't long before she noticed him and looked up with big doe eyes full of tears, "I'm terribly sorry for making a public spectacle." she apologized.

"No, no. It is I who should apologize for intruding. If you'll pardon me for asking is there anything I can do to help?" he offered sincerely, for he had a kind heart.

"No, I'm afraid there is nothing anyone can do to help us. You don't want to get involved."

"At least tell me what's got you so upset and let me decide if I want to get involved."

"My little girl is in the hospital and my other daughter is safe for now. I must go."

"What happened? I mean, will she be alright?"

"I... I don't know. She has a broken arm and a broken rib. The doctors said her lung was punctured and they have her in surgery right now. I had to find a place I could be alone to think things through." She said through soul wrenching sobs.

"How did this happen? Was it a car accident?"

It was at this point that the emotional flood gates opened and the distraught woman poured out her story. It was a tale of fear and violence. An ex-husband and father that brow beat her and her children threatening them with a gun. However, it didn't stop at threats. There were beating, choking and slashing incidents. She had lost track of the number of trips to the hospital.

She had tried to run but he always found them and the violence would be worse each time and she was now in fear for her children's lives as well as her own. She was afraid that if he killed her there would be no one to protect Cornett and Chrystal. "Please, I must go. He'll be looking for us. Thank you for listening but you must not involve yourself. It'll only make things worse." she pleaded as she turned to leave.

"I can help... I don't even know your name."

"Brandy. My name is Brandy D. Canter. Now I really must go." she called over her shoulder as she began to hurry away.

He watched her go realizing that wanting to help and possessing the right skills to be able to help were two vastly different sets of circumstances. This life event was to be his inspiration for his chosen path in life.

Later he would graduate Cambridge law school with a first, Yale Law school top of his class and receiving his Masters Business Administration from London School of Business. During his life at Yale he had been tapped for the Skull and Bones and had been a well respected Bonesman. He had learned many valuable secrets and made many powerful and strategic connections.

He never forgot that day in the Edinburgh park. He had been preparing himself, honing his skills and developing his very extensive network. He was ready.

A decade and a half of performing his magic on behalf of innocent people hopelessly trapped in dangerous circumstances had slipped by. He was tired, bone tired. He had witnessed so much anguish and desperation and had successfully liberated each and every one, young and old, rich and poor but now it was time. Time for him to wind down before the stress took its toll. Yet how could he turn his back on so many, and numbers were growing, when he had the skill set and alliances that could set them free and give them new lives.

He would, he thought, revisit his personal issues but for now he was on his way to meet another of life's casualties. They were to meet at Terry's Gentlemen's Club. One of the oldest and most exclusive of the gentlemen's clubs, established in 1691. This members only haven of serenity and enclave of tradition is situated in a grand Portland stone Grade I listed building secreted away in Piccadilly.

He felt comfortable in his handmade pale grey wool and silk pinhead suit, white poplin shirt crafted of the finest Italian cotton with mother of pearl buttons and classic full brogue oxford shoes hand made from the finest calf leather. Standing six foot two inches tall with silver hair and electric blue eyes he truly made an imposing figure.

Entering the front doors he was greeted by the doorman, "Good morning sir."

"Ah, good morning, my good man. It's a fine morning."

"It is indeed, sir."

"How's the family, George?"

"Everyone's fine, sir. Thank you for asking. Susie wants to know when we'll see you for dinner again?"

"Tell her I look forward to her toad in the hole with mustard onion gravy.

Would you have Mr. Andropov sent to my private room, please George?"

"Right you are sir."

Inside is smart and surprisingly brightly lit, with men reading newspapers in arm chairs. He made his way to his reserved room to await Picov Andropov.

He had used this room in his club many times over the years. Extensive precautions had been take to ensure complete privacy. During construction the walls, ceilings and floors of theses rooms had all been made sound proof and he always swept the room for any kind of cameras or listening devices before a meeting.

Tea had been arranged and they settled in with their cuppa. Picov began by saying, "You come very highly recommended, indeed, Mr. Wolf."

Benjamin only smiled appreciatively. "What seems to be troubling you, Mr. Andropov?" In fact, he already knew what had the Russian trucking magnate so upset. He had done his homework. He always knew more about the victim's circumstance than even they knew themselves but felt it was important for them to share their story.

Picov concluded with, "My family and I are being threatened by the

Bratva[1]. I can't hold them off much longer and I don't know what to do to protect my family."

"I am going to give you an address and I want you to remember it. I want you to take your family to that address and await further instructions." Ben handed Picov a burner phone instructing him that neither he nor any member of his family was to contact anyone. And so the prestidigitation begins and hence Benjamin Wolf was dubbed the 'Illusionist'.

First order of business, remove the target from harm's way. Second neutralize the threat and finally eliminate the threat.

It took several long months but the siege was finally purged and the family could return to their lives. It was time once again for the Illusionist to consider retiring the mantle.

---

[1] AKA russkaya mafiya or Russian mafia sometimes referred to as brotherhood

2 BEN GOES FOR A WALK

Day 1

His bedroom was awash with the pale glow of the morning sun not yet above the horizon. Stirring and shaking off the last vestiges of sleep he emerged from his bed stretching and yawning as if breaking free from his warm, cosy cocoon. Ben showered, shaved, dressed in khaki hiking shorts and t-shirt, put on comfortable walking shoes and prepared himself a hearty breakfast of multigrain toast, granola and coffee. Setting the security alarm on the house he then threw his pack over his shoulder and out the door he strode leaving his cares behind, he hoped.

Looking down as he stepped out he spotted a footprint in the garden underneath the kitchen window as if someone had been peering in. Turning he locked the door and set off secure in the knowledge that anyone breaking in would set off the alarm bringing the police. The day was in its infancy and he was not about to let dodgy unseen forces throw a spanner in the works.

Checking his watch told him it was 07:00 as he made his way to the old Keswick to Penrith rail line walking trail. The air was fresh and cool, the grass covered with dew and the songs of the robins and blue birds buoyed up his spirits.

He hiked briskly along the old rail bed enjoying the colours and textures of the surrounding landscape. It wasn't long before he reached one of his planned diversions. A long forgotten and tumbled down yet largely intact abbey that he had wanted to see lay a short distance off his planned route.

The landscape transformed from an easy walking abandoned rail bed to rocky and hilly terrain. He could hear woodland creatures going about their daily activities in the undergrowth on either side of the trail. The sound of rustling dry leaves and every once in awhile the snapping of a twig and, of course, the constant cheerful bird songs.

Cresting a small knoll he caught a glimpse of the abbey perched on the summit of a lush green hill dotted with wild flowers beyond. It would be a steep climb but he had been assured that the view would be worth the effort not to mention the satisfaction of exploring the old abbey. If his information was correct ancient relics could still be found in the ruins.

He had thought himself fit but the climb was certainly putting him to the test. Finally at the top he stood in front of the huge wooden door to the abbey. After battling with the sharp, clawing brambles, that seemed bent on shredding his clothes and flesh, and wrestling in a herculean struggle against stout vines that had taken over the old ruin, he put his well muscled shoulder to the massive door finally penetrating to the inner sanctum. It was as if the monks had simply gotten up and left. There were pewter tankards, plates, tables, chairs, all of the ordinary things one associates with everyday living just lying about as they had been so many years ago.

Ben had felt as though he was being watched ever since he had left his cottage that morning. Nothing concrete just that creepy feeling but it was even stronger here in the ruins. He climbed the well worn stone stairs up to what remained of the upper floor. Looking out he stood in rapt silence as his senses drank in the grand vista spread before him like a banquet for the eyes. He devoured the picturesque patchwork of valleys and fells blanketed in shamrock green meadows enhanced by random displays of pink and purple heather. The magnificent tapestry was the better for its leafy woodlands and sparkling gems of sapphire lakes. Then scarcely noticeable the click clicking of a tiny pebble as it fell and ricocheted its way to the floor. Startled Ben looked about but could find nothing to have caused the dislodging of the pebble. Perhaps it was the ghost of the abbey? Anyroad, unnerved he descended hurriedly to the ground and back down the steep hillside to the rail line to resume his trek. Upon reaching the path he was jostled violently by an overtaking cyclist who disappeared within seconds around a bend in the rail trail. Shaken but not stirred he regained his composure, dusted himself off and continued his journey without giving the incident a second thought.

He stopped in the tiny hamlet of Troutbeck, midway between Keswick and Penrith for lunch. It is a tranquil village Nestled in a valley on the banks of the Trout Beck[2] cradled by the slopes of Wansfell and Applethwaite Common.

Entering the Quiet Man pub he ordered a ploughman's, a pint the local beer and took his repast to a table on the patio. He hardly noticed when shortly after his arrival a solitary cyclist pulled in and dismounting the bicycle with their back to Ben disappearing hastily into the pub.

Polishing off the last morsels of freshly baked bread, delicious locally produced cheddar cheese, pickled onion and washing it down with the last swallow of local brew he threw his pack over his shoulder and began the last half of his days journey to Penrith where he would spend the night.

Ben, eager to be on his way, was blissfully unaware of the mystery cyclist's departure from the pub immediately after his own. He whistled a jaunty tune as he trod the rail bed enroute to his next target, that of Dacre Castle. Castles, their history and magic were his passions.

Dacre Castle was constructed in the 14th century, a pele tower with walls sixty-six feet high and seven feet thick, as protection against the Scots. With Scottish raiding on the decline in the 17th century the castle was renovated by the fifth Lord Dacre to be more habitable by the addition of large windows. However, with his death in 1715 his possessions were sold off and the castle changed hands several times and fell into a state of disrepair until today when it has been restored and is open to the public.

---

[2] Mountain stream

His hike to Dacre Castle was happily uneventful. At long last, he could actually begin to feel the stress melting away with each mile.

Great Britain seems awash with spooks in a variety of manifestations and Dacre Castle had its fair share. The castle was the meeting place of three kings attempting to orchestrate a peace treaty between England and Scotland. The ghosts of the three remorseful kings are said to roam the castle.

In the 15th century Sir Guy Dacre fell madly in love with Eloise, the daughter of a French Nobleman. But this was not to be a story of idyllic love but a tale of obsession and sadistic retribution. Alas she rebuffed his advances. Enlisting the help of his tutor to win her affections. Regrettably the tutor fell victim to her charms and an affair soon began whilst Sir Guy was away in Scotland fighting, however, upon his return Eloise agreed to marry him. Still blissfully unaware of the affair Sir Guy was once again off to Scotland enlisting his loyal friend Lyulph to look after the castle. It was then that Lyulph discovered the deception. The lovers, knowing their deceit would be exposed, left the castle.

Upon Sir Guy's return Lyulph informed him of the sordid treachery. Whereupon Sir Guy pursued and took Eloise prisoner locking her in the dark castle dungeon. Eloise soon noticed her lover was chained to the wall of her cell but when she sought to kiss him, his head rolled from his shoulders.

Eloise was held captive in the cell with the rotting corpse of her lover until she went mad and died. It is said that tragically their ghosts are destined to walk the halls of Dacre Castle to this very day.

He had just turned up the path to the castle when the cyclist sped by unobserved by Ben. He was suitably impressed with the guided tour of the castle and thanking his guide set out for Penrith.

Arriving at the Bide-A-While Bed and Breakfast just outside Penrith after a ramble without incident.

Day 2

Setting out from Penrith his next stop Dalemain (Manor in the valley) Estates with its finely dressed pink stone Georgian facade behind the ordered geometry of its Palladian architecture. Inside he marvelled at the confusion of winding passages, quaint stairways and unexpected rooms. There was the Fretwork room displaying a magnificent 16th century plaster ceiling with beautiful oak panelling and the Chinese room with its original 18th century, hand painted wallpaper, riotously alive with birds, insects and flowers.

After enjoying his visit to Dalemain Estates he resumed his walk stopping at the Stone the Crows Pub in Rolling Downs for a ploughman's and a pint of scrumpy.

Out on the lawn some raucous crows were demanding scraps from the pub patrons. One of the lunchtime customers sitting not far from Ben was speculating to her friend on what one would call a group of crows. "I suppose like most birds they would be a flock" and her friend rejoined, "No. I think there is a different term for crows like geese. A group of geese is a gaggle."

Ben leaned over to the pair and offered, "I'm sorry, I don't mean to be rude but I couldn't help overhearing your debate. A group of crows is generically called a flock but technically termed a murder of crows[3]. Many people view the appearance of crows as an omen of death. They're thought to circle in large numbers above sites where animals or people are expected to soon die."

"How very interesting. Thank you for your help."

While Ben was enjoying his lunch, the cheerful sounds of the pub and village life, the mysterious cyclist was not far away paying a deadly visit to someone in Rolling Downs.

Then it was on to the Hide-A-Way bed and breakfast in the village of Glenridding on Ullswater. He enjoyed a delicious meal of fresh pan fried trout, tatties for befores and spotted dick for afters.

Ben was pleasantly exhausted and turned in early so he could make an early start Saturday morning.

---

[3] There are several possible origins for the term based on old folk tales and superstitions. One such folk tale is that crows will gather and decide the capital fate of another crow.

3 WOLF AMONG SHEEP

The fragrant meadow grass, sweet perfume of the wild flowers and fulsome smell of the warm earth beneath his feet filled his senses. Wisps of fine dust, like puffs of smoke, drifted and fell with each step as he trod the narrow winding path. He felt at peace for the first time in what seemed an eternity.

He had been walking since early morning on a breakfast of a bacon butty and steaming cup of coffee. His stomach was beginning to grumble.

Benjamin Wolf, moved his six foot two inch athletic frame gracefully along the path. An Illusionist of sorts, Benjamin had a special gift for making things disappear, reappear and even transform them into distinctly dissimilar entities. His ingenious talent was his innate ability to hide items of incalculable wealth in plain sight.

His extraordinarily exclusive international list of exceedingly wealthy clients included some very powerful and dangerous people. Ben did not deal directly with the property personally. He would put in motion, through ultra-discreet communications, the form, strategy, means of transport and contacts necessary for the implementation leaving no trace of his involvement.

It was little things at first. Trivial events such as a mere prolonged glance in his direction in a restaurant or seeing the same person on more than one occasion in the same day. Ben was a creature of habit and fastidious in his personal space, a place for everything and everything in its place, as a result he began to notice small things out of place.

It was this seemingly innocuous series of occurrences that were an element of the impetus for Ben's walking holiday.

Ascending a gentle knoll a village began to emerge as if rising up from the depths of terra firma. First the tip of the church steeple, then the bell tower beneath and slowly the tiny, ancient village of Toadspool in the Dell, nestled sleepily in a secluded valley, came into view. Crossing over a humped back stone bridge that looked like a remnant of Roman architecture, he could hear the echoes below of his footfalls on the well worn wooden planks.

He was to spend a few days with an old friend and past client, Sebastian Monk, Earl of Uppington on the Downs. The reluctant Earl's stately manor house, Monks Hall, commanded a panoramic view of the surrounding hillsides and valley below.

He was looking forward to a hot bath and a meal. There was an eerie stillness as he walked along the high street of Toadspool in the Dell. It had the ghostly feel of an abandoned village and yet he felt as though he was being watched. There were no curious faces peering out from cottage windows at a stranger passing through, no typical activity in the local post office, no inquisitive canines roaming the streets and not a sound emanated from The Befores & Afters pub.

Glancing about the unnaturally quiet village as he walked he spotted the grill of a shiny new black Venitia Z 200 Roadster parked surreptitiously behind the village hall. A flash of motion in an alleyway caught his attention but was so fleeting he could not be certain of what he saw.

Leaving the creepy village behind and starting the steep climb up to Monks Hall a fire engine red Jaguar XKE with its top down and radio blaring seemed on a collision course with his knees causing him to dive for cover. He scrambled out of the ditch but not fast enough to see the driver or make out the number plate.

Ben could feel the temperature drop a few degrees as he entered the dappled sunlight of the dense forest of ancient oaks and yews. The road wound its way steadily upward and deeper into the forest that seemed to wrap itself about him. The smell of damp, decomposing vegetation permeated the air around him. The scurrying sounds of forest creatures could be heard always just out of sight or was there something else traversing the shadows of the forest parallel to his movements? He was getting the jitters it was probably just his imagination.

Finally he broke free of the oppressive woods into the sunlight and out onto the luxuriant, green of well manicured, sprawling lawns. His friend Sebastian awaited him on the steps of the grand entrance. "Benjamin, you've been missed. It's been such a long time since you were my guest at Monks Hall."

The pair embraced and Benjamin responded, "Far too long my friend."

As was his custom, Jarvis appeared silently at their elbows as if from thin air asking, "Can I help you with that Mr. Wolf?" referring to Benjamin's rucksack. The butler believed in tradition and was attired in black tie, grey vest, white wing collar dress shirt, black morning coat, white gloves and grey striped trousers.

"Jarvis, it's good to see you. I'm glad to see you haven't lost your gift of stealth. You seem to always know the exact moment and location your services are required."

Jarvis relieved Ben of his knapsack saying, "I've taken the liberty of running a hot bath for you sir. Drinks have been dispensed in the drawing room and I've arranged for yours to be waiting for you in the bath, Mr. Wolf.

Dinner will be served in one hour in the main dining room."

"Thank you Jarvis."

The trio entered Monks Hall where the Earl said, "I look forward to catching up. I'll leave you in Jarvis' care."

Ben followed the exceedingly efficient butler upstairs to his room.

"Will that be all, sir?" enquired Jarvis.

"Yes, Jarvis. Thank you. Oh, Jarvis. Can you tell me who was driving the bright red Jaguar that arrived just before me?"

"That would be Duchess Cassandra, sir."

'Probably middle aged trying to regain her youth with fast cars and fast lifestyle. Not to mention always used to getting her own way.' he thought as he took a long draft of his icy cold beer before slipping into his hot bath. He tried to let all his cares float away but he couldn't shake off the sensation that someone was rummaging around in his life.

Alighting from his bath he shaved and stepping into his bedroom he was surprised to find, laid out on his bed, Hugo Boss dinner attire and accessories. Completing the ensemble with Charles Tyrwhitt shoes and all a perfect fit. He dressed and made his way to dinner.

Sebastian, his waistcoat buttons bravely straining against his rotund figure, and his guests were gathered in a sumptuously decorated drawing room. The walls were lined in bolection-moulded walnut panelling and furnished in luxurious, overstuffed sofas and chairs. Paintings by old Masters hung as if they had always belonged there.

Entering the drawing room Ben was greeted cordially by his host, a nattily dressed Sebastian Monk wearing a red velvet smoking jacket and gold silk ascot. "I trust you are feeling refreshed and in need of nourishment, both for the body and the intellect. Let me introduce you to my guests." Sebastian called for the attention of the three other guests gathered in the drawing room to make introductions.

"Lady and gentlemen this is my very good friend Benjamin Wolf. He's... a Master Illusionist of sorts."

This made Benjamin uncomfortable causing him to smile awkwardly.

"Benjamin, may I present the stunning Duchess Cassandra Webb, Duchess of Camelot. You are looking particularly beautiful this evening, Duchess Cassandra." an auburn haired beauty with flashing emerald green eyes. Ben was smitten the moment he looked into those emerald green eyes. He was lost in their depths.

She was captivating in a sensually sculptured black, stretch knit mini dress from Balmain finished with sheer panels of lace complimented by Giavanito Rossi Portofino black leather open toed sandals with four inch spiked heels.

Benjamin was abruptly nonplussed as he realized she was the recklessly wild driver in the fire engine red Jaguar that had nearly cut his life short. She was the most beautiful woman he had ever had the great pleasure to lay eyes on. He found himself mesmerised as he stammered, "Y...you almost ran me down earlier today!"

The pair locked eyes as if in a trance. The chemistry between them was palpable.

Duchess Cassandra blushed ever so slightly and smiling sheepishly replied, "Dear me. I do apologise for the near miss. I must learn to be more careful in future."

Ben couldn't be entirely certain she wasn't expressing regret for having missed him.

Sebastian continued, "Ahem... Err... Yes well. Moving on. The gentleman leaning nonchalantly on the mantle is international real estate mogul, who I'm sure you recognise from his pictures in the tabloids, Ulysses Upman." Ulysses, looking dapper in his Dolce & Gabbana three piece wool-silk blend tuxedo trimmed in satin with cloth covered buttons and a crisp white shirt complete the picture of sophistication, stood looking aloof as he rolled his talisman, a gold sovereign, across his knuckles as was his habit.

Ben nodded his acknowledgement.

"Finally, I'd like you to meet world renowned Doctor of Philosophy, Professor I. M. Boring."

Ben looked at the potty looking Professor in a tatty white polyester blend dinner jacket, plaid polyester slacks and pink trainers. He thought to himself, "There's more to this fellow than meets the eye."

"Oh, bollocks!" exclaimed Boring.

"Whatever seems to be the matter Professor?" asked Sebastian.

"I seem to have lost my glasses. This simply won't do. It won't do at all."

"If you'll pardon me Professor." interjected Ben. "They're on your head."

"Oh...oh yes. Thank you... um... ur. I'm sorry. Have we met?"

Sebastian, his patience wearing thin, reintroduced Benjamin, "Professor, if you would be so kind as to attend me. This is my very good friend Benjamin Wolf, a Master Illusionist of sorts."

"Ah, a Master Illusionist you say. How very interesting. Did you realize that Illusionists create a kind of perceptual and aesthetic experience that traditional philosophers have largely ignored? In fact..."

"Yes, I'm sure that's a fascinating topic. For another time perhaps, Professor." interrupted Sebastian somewhat irritably.

Ben nodded his salutation to the eccentric Professor and returned his attention to the captivating Duchess Cassandra.

"We were expecting one more guest, Chrystal D. Canter, daughter of the matriarch of one of the oldest Cognac producing families in Europe, to join us for dinner but it seems she has been delayed.

Jarvis entered the drawing room announcing that dinner was served.

Ben offered his arm to the Duchess who looked at him a little coquettishly before allowing herself to be escorted into dinner. He observed the look of petulance on the real estate mogul's face when Duchess Cassandra accepted his arm.

Entering the opulent dining room Jarvis seated Duchess Cassandra then selected the chair to her right, "May I sir?" he said with a sly wink as he seated him much to the chagrin of Ulysses Upman.

"You may, indeed, Jarvis. Thank you." Ben acknowledged as he sat down looking especially pleased with himself.

Ulysses immediately took the seat directly opposite the Duchess and catching her eye said, "Fascinating. I've been looking at your eyes all afternoon, because I've never seen such dark eyes with so much light in them."

Ignoring his cheesy remark the Duchess turned to Ben, "Now that was magic. Do you know any other tricks?" quipped Duchess Cassandra demurely.

Ben placed an unusual coin on the table in front of him announcing he would push it through the table. The Professor interrupted by observing, "Excuse me, Mr. Wolf, but that is a very unusual coin you have there. I believe that symbol is and ancient triskelion, is it not?"

"Yes, yes, Professor. That is correct. Now if I may continue?" Next placing his napkin over the salt cellar he put it on top of the coin. He removed the covered salt cellar to reveal the coin was still there and finally he covered the coin again then pressing down rapidly and firmly on the salt cellar collapsing the napkin and appearing to push the cellar through the table. He brought his hand from beneath the table revealing the salt cellar and apologizing, "Cor! I guess I don't know my own strength."

This sleight of hand was greeted with a round of applause and look of astonishment on Duchess Cassandra's face.

Sebastian proclaimed, "Brilliant! You never cease to amaze me my friend. Now let's make this delicious meal that Chef has prepared for us disappear before it gets cold."

They were treated to a delicious repast, fine wine and engaging conversation.

Dr. Boring, clearly inspired by Benjamin's coin, expounded on the triskelion and its philosophical significance. "The three legs of the triskelion or triskele refer to motion, evolution and illumination. Illuminationist Philosophy started in twelfth century Persia and has been an important force in Islamic philosophy. Illuminationists put forward a view of reality in which essence is more important than existence, and intuitive knowledge more significant than scientific knowledge. They draw on the notion of light as a way to delve into the relationship between God, the Light of Lights, and His creation. Thus resulting in the view that reality as a whole is a continuum, with the physical world being an aspect of the divine."

Professor I. M. Boring seemed not to notice that no one appeared to be listening.

Ben had just called the Duchess, Duchess Cassandra, for the third time when she turned to him saying, "Please just call me Cassandra or Cassie."

To which he thanked her, "As you wish, Duch... Uh, I mean Cassandra. That is a very beautiful name. It means, in Greek, shining upon man and in Christian, helper of mankind. It is said Cassandra had the gift of prophesy."

"Yes but she was cursed. No one would believe her prophecies." countered Duchess Cassandra.

The pudding had just been served when Jarvis appeared beside Sebastian and whispered something in his master's ear. A look of dismay on Sebastian's face told everyone it was bad news. He excused himself and left the room.

A short time later Sebastian returned to the dining room looking gutted and paused before speaking, silence fell around the table as he announced, "Something terrible has happened. I've just received word that Chrystal D. Canter has gone missing.

Duchess Cassandra stifled a gasp raising her wine glass to her lips to conceal her dismay.

I called her home and her secretary said she left three hours ago. It is only an hour's drive from her home to Monks Hall so I had Jarvis put a call through to the police. They've just called to inform me that they found her automobile abandoned in Dead End Lane on the outskirts of Toadspool in the Dell. There were no signs of a struggle."

The party finished their afters in silence and Sebastian suggested they adjourn to the drawing room for coffee and brandy.

Dr. Boring had cornered Ulysses Upman and was enthusiastically trying to convince him how wonderfully exhilarating Philosophical Rationalism was. Ulysses eyes had glazed over immediately after the good Doctor uttered the word "Philosophical".

Ben suggested a walk in the garden to Cassandra who accepted with pleasure. They strolled amicably about the lavish flower beds and astonishing topiaries. He searched for an intelligent and engaging topic of conversation in vain. He wanted to know everything about her but didn't want to look like a love sick school boy.

Before he could form composed, coherent subject matter she asked, "Where could she have gone? She wouldn't have left her car of her own volition, surely."

"It does seem odd.

How long have you known Sebastian?" Ben asked, trying to turn the conversation to more pleasant thoughts.

"Not long.

Do you think she could have gotten out of her car to go for a leisurely walk and gotten lost? Those woods are quite thick. Perhaps she tripped and twisted an ankle or maybe she fell and struck her head? She could be laying out there in the cold damp forest wondering if anyone will find her." her anxiety beginning to increase with her imagination.

"Cassie, I'm sure that the police are doing everything in their power to find her and bring her to safety." he said a trifle impatiently.

"Do forgive me, Ben, but it's been a long day I think I'll turn in for the night." she said, stifling a yawn.

"Of course, Cassandra. I'll walk you to your room." he replied disappointedly.

The pair made their way companionably back to the house in silence. Cassandra was deep in thought as she bid Ben goodnight at the door to her room.

Ben went in search of a nightcap and a book. He found Sebastian in the library enjoying a brandy. Over his host's shoulder he noticed the patio doors carefully closing.

"May I offer you a nightcap, Ben?" his host offered, holding out a crystal decanter to fill his glass.

"Just the ticket. I see you have a very extensive library. I thought I might borrow one of your copies of Agatha Christie to help me sleep."

"Help yourself, old chap. They're all first editions.

I shall not be joining you for brunch. The police want to interview me bright and early tomorrow morning. Please pass my regrets on to the others and I will join you when I can."

4 ULYSSES UPMAN

"And lead us not into temptation, but deliver us from the evil one." - Matthew 6:13

Ulysses Upman had poured himself a snifter of brandy and stepped outside to the patio for a pipe of tobacco. The air was crisp and cool. A gentle breeze played happily among the grasses and trees creating animated shadows and sounds as if the night was filled with wild things.

At just thirty-seven years of age, a reputed playboy he was always looking for new conquests. If he had just had more time he could have added Duchess Cassandra to his trophy list. He didn't have a member of the aristocracy yet.

Why had he come he wondered? He didn't like Sebastian, in fact truth be told, he feared him. He could have just sent his pound of flesh and avoided the aggro.

If only he hadn't succumbed to temptation that one time. Those innocent people would still be alive and he'd be free. One moment of weakness and he had been enslaved.

It had been fifteen years ago and his first major project, a shopping mall with one hundred and thirty-five stores and underground parking. The project had been delayed and construction costs had ballooned to the level where he would be bankrupt before he finished the job. He was at his lowest point when he was approached by a syndicate with a solution. They would supply him with all of the construction supplies at a discounted rate if he agreed to sign an exclusive contract with their firm.

He had been a mug[4]. He should have known then that the materials were noddy[5] but he had turned a blind eye. The project was completed. The commercial spaces filled, the mall thrived and his real estate development company grew faster than he could dream. Life was good for almost two years before disaster struck.

He could remember the moment vividly when his assistant burst into his office in London crying profusely and saying between her tears, "It's a nightmare. People dead." That's when his phones began to ring. First the Malaysian police next the fire department, then the media all wanting a piece of him.

Malaysian authorities wanted to extradite him but he had applied a few bungs[6] in the right places and finally it all went away, for him but not for the victims.

News never seemed to reach Great Britain and his business flourished at home, the continent and in North America. He was a very wealthy man, a billionaire, in fact. Until about seven years ago, a few days after his thirtieth birthday he received an invitation to Monks Hall. Flattered by an invitation from the Earl of Uppington on the Downs and more than a little curious he had accepted. It was then he had learned the Earl's ulterior motive of extortion.

The Earl, Sebastian Monk, had somehow learned of his grim secret and would now use it to enslave him.

It had been seven long years of being a host for a blood sucking parasite and now his tormenter was tightening the screws. Now he wanted to be made

---

[4] gullible person
[5] inferior
[6] bribes

a silent partner in his business! The business he had worked so hard to build.

5 CASSIE INVESTIGATES

Duchess Cassandra, holding her breath, closed her bedroom door and waited quietly listening to Benjamin's footsteps fade as he withdrew to another part of the vast house. She slowly opened her door a crack to search the dimly lit upper hallway for any signs of life. Once she was certain there was no one around she slipped out of her room making her way quickly and quietly down the ornate Edwardian oak staircase, out the patio doors and across the lawn to her car.

Sliding behind the hand rubbed mahogany steering wheel, into the glove leather bucket seat she held her breath as she turned the ignition on the precision built Jaguar. The powerful twelve cylinder engine came to life on the first crank, purring like a contented kitten. She rolled unnoticed down the drive and gained the forest road proceeding directly to Dead End Lane.

Coming to a stop in a lay-by, where a piece of yellow tape left behind by the police fluttered in the breeze, she removed a flashlight from the car's glove box and alighted from the Jag. The abandoned car had been removed to an impound lot which didn't leave much in the way of options to search. She surveyed the ground and surrounding area. Next she studied the ditch and forest edge for any clue as to whether or not the missing Decanter heiress had, in fact, entered the woods and if so where she had entered. It was impossible to detect any disturbances in the vicinity due to the trampled mess left by the local P.C. Plod patrol.

She walked slowly along the road scanning the tree line for anything out of place. Was that a flash of motion deep in the shadows or did she imagine it?

A deafening clap of thunder startled her distracting her from her quest. Huge drops of rain began to pelt down forcing Cassandra to run for the cover of the Jag. Crestfallen she returned to Monks Hall where she was able to get inside and up to her room unobserved, or so she thought. She hurried to get out of her wet clothes and into a warm, dry nightdress. It was gone eleven when she dozed off.

Benjamin rose early the following morning making his way hurriedly first to the library and then to the drawing room where he located his objective. He picked up The Toadspool Journal and The Sunday Times and scanned the front pages. Satisfied there was no mention of his name he glanced around nervously. He then moved on to the dining room where he found the others gathered for brunch and upon arrival he announced, "Good morning Lady and gentlemen. Sebastian sends his regrets that he could not join us for brunch but his presence was required at the police station for an interview."

A full English of grilled sausages, golden fried potatoes, toast, fried tomatoes, rashers of sizzling bacon, steaming porridge, kippers and five kinds of farm fresh eggs: scrambled, fried, poached, boiled and Benedict, as well as fresh fruit, was laid out on the sideboard for the guests to help themselves.

Duchess Cassandra stepped over to the sideboard and nibbling on a warm slice of buttered toast with savoury gooseberry and heady aromatic elderflower preserves retrieved the local morning broadsheet. The headline read 'Canter Brandy Heiress Missing' and halfway down the front page another headline 'Unexplained Death of Trucking Giant'. The latter reported that the Russian owner of the largest cargo company in Britain, Picov Andropov, had been found mysteriously murdered in his country house in Rolling Downs, Cumbria Friday afternoon.

"I don't know what this world is coming to with all of these killings and this one even in the victim's own home. Your ramble must have taken you through Rolling Downs on your way here?" she commented pointing out the article concerning the murder of two days prior.

"Why y...yes. I guess you're right. Tea Cassandra?" He turned ashen and was visibly shaken by the news but tried desperately not to let on that he recognized the victim.

"Yes, thank you Ben." Cassandra, not failing to notice his anxiety, accepted the tea Ben offered.

Boring began, "To understand death we need to understand life in some detail, since death occurs when a life ends. If life were a simple matter of automata like pocket watches ticking away time, death would be an equally simple matter. We would die when motion ceases.

Consider that we are conscious beings. According to the higher brain standard, human death is the irreversible cessation of the capacity for consciousness. We humans..."

"Yes, yes, alright. I'm sure you may find this all very interesting but I find it both tedious and morbid. Can we not find a more cheerful topic for discussion?" complained Ulysses Upman.

An uncomfortable silence fell over the little group. Just then the darkness of the overcast morning was split by a brilliant flash of lightening startling everyone. The glare from the lightening illuminated a tall figure on the lawn half turned towards the house and beside him what appeared to be a great grey wolf at the edge of the forest, for a split second. So fleetingly, in fact, Cassandra could not be certain of what she saw. The great booming bass of the resulting thunder shook the house to its foundations.

Suddenly the lights went out in the dining room and everyone froze. Then just as suddenly the lights came on and each of the guests relaxing, breathed a sigh of relief. However, they all jumped when Sebastian spoke from the open doorway, "Well, that was an experience I would not like to have to repeat.

How was brunch? Uneventful I trust?"

They all spoke at once sounding like a babble of conversation.

"Good." said Sebastian as he sat down at the table.

Jarvis seemed to materialize in the room at his master's elbow enquiring, "May I have the cook prepare something for you, sir?"

To which Sebastian replied, "No, no, thank you Jarvis. I'll just have something from the buffet."

"Very good sir. Will there be anything else M' Lord?"

The guests all stood around awkwardly and somewhat expectantly as if waiting to be dismissed by the headmaster until Ben suggested, "Shall we adjourn to the drawing room with our coffee and let Sebastian enjoy his repast in peace. I'm sure we're all eager to hear about his experience but all things in due course." and with that the little group trouped into the drawing room to await Sebastian and his tales from the interrogation. The room was cosy with crackling fires in each of the fireplaces at either end of the room.

The first to speak after they had all settled themselves in comfy chairs with their coffee was Ulysses, "She's probably made spur of the moment alternate plans and was picked up by some dashing, married man to spend the weekend."

"Is that what you think? I can see how your mind works.

If she wanted to advertise to the world she was having an illicit affair and snub Sebastian Monk, Earl of Uppington on the Downs, one of her families oldest friends." retorted Duchess Cassandra.

The philosopher tried his hand at conciliation, "Relationships are the quintessential common denominator we all have in common. They define our lives and persistently shape, for better or worse, the quality of our lives.

What I'm trying to say is if you go out looking for friends, you are going to find they are very scarce. If you go out to be a friend, you will find them everywhere."

"Very profound indeed, Professor." concurred Ben.

Duchess Cassandra had moved to the window looking out on the lawns. She was deep in thought as she searched the tree line for any sign of the mysterious figure she thought she had spotted. She peered through the darkness and torrential rain and was blinded by the sporadic flashes of lightening but try as she might there was no sign of the extraordinary apparition. Perhaps it had been her imagination playing tricks or had she witnessed a kidnapper?

Her train of thought was broken when Sebastian entered the drawing room expressing regret for his absence, "I am terribly sorry for my absence this morning. I do hope you will all remain as my guests for one more night?

I was, as you are aware, unavoidably detained by the police. They seemed to be under the misapprehension that I might know something about Chrystal D. Canter's mysterious disappearance which, of course, is nonsense.

They questioned me for some time and finally decided that unfortunately either I could or would offer them no further illumination on her whereabouts.

I was left with the distinct impression that despite all my protestations the local constable still thought I was withholding information."

"Were you? I mean do you know something about Ms. Canter? You are among friends Sebastian." asked Duchess Cassandra.

"Well... ahem. There have been rumours of certain, um... indiscretions, shall we say."

"What sort of rumours?" enquired Cassandra eagerly.

"Harrumph... Well... um...ur Ungentlemanly, what, what? I've heard she has a married fancy man somewhere in the vicinity. That's all I know. Now I suppose you'll call the police and spill the beans." groused Sebastian.

"See I told you so." said Ulysses triumphantly, feeling vindicated.

"No, but you will, Sir Sebastian. It is your duty as a citizen and a peer." admonished Duchess Cassandra ignoring Ulysses' remark.

"Oh, well, since you put it like that." Sebastian whinged. Turning on his heel he left the drawing room to make a call to the police from his library.

Outside the storm had passed and the sun had finally made a dazzling appearance. Water droplets on the tips of leaves and grass glinted like millions of tiny diamonds. Humidity rose from the wet grass and pavement in visible steamy waves.

Duchess Cassandra announced, "I think I'll go for a walk."

"Would you care for some company, Duchess Cassandra?" offered Ulysses Upman.

"Fine. If you'll excuse me I must go up to my room to put on proper walking shoes." she replied somewhat petulantly.

"I'll wait here for you shall I?" responded Ulysses eagerly.

Professor Boring attempted to engage Ben in a philosophical discussion about money, "Have you ever thought about the social influences of money, Mr. Wolf?" He continued without waiting for a response, "Social philosopher, Georg Simmel did. His outlook, while gloomy, is not wholly negative. He postulated that as money and transactions increased, the independence of the individual decreases as they are drawn into a holistic network of exchange governed by quantifiable monetary value. Paradoxically, this results in greater freedom of choice for the individual, as money can be deployed toward any possible goal. Thus money's homogenizing nature encourages greater liberty and equality.

What do you think, Mr. Wolf?"

"I think "'The love of money is the root of all evil;' Timothy Chapter six, verse ten. And I think I need a drink and some fresh air, Professor." Ben rejoined testily.

Cassandra had parted company with Ulysses when he had rudely taken a business call shortly after their walk had begun. She now found herself at the edge of the forest where she thought she had seen the mysterious figure and the magnificent wolf. Surveying the area she could find no lingering discernible trace of anyone or anything having stood there and looking intently into the forest shadows she could find no sign of their presence. Who was this curious creature and what was he up to? Had she actually seen a man and a wolf standing companionably in the driving rain or had it been a trick of the storm?

Deep in her thoughts she made her way back to the house for four o'clock cocktails. En route she met Ulysses who, by this time, had finished his phone call at last and they walked to the drawing room together. Upon entering the drawing room they were greeted by Benjamin, drink in hand.

"May I offer the wandering twosome cocktails?" he cajoled mockingly.

"Has anyone seen Sebastian?" asked Duchess Cassandra.

"Not me." replied Ulysses.

"Have you seen him, Ben?" asked Cassandra uneasily.

"No. I haven't seen him since he went to the library to call the police. Have either of you seen Professor Boring?" answered Ben.

"Um... oh... Did I hear my name mentioned?" asked the Professor sleepily from the chesterfield facing the window.

"Sorry Professor. We didn't notice you napping. Just how long have you been there?" said Benjamin.

"I sat down here right after everyone left and the sun made me sleepy so I thought I'd rest my eyes awhile and the next thing I knew I was hearing my name. I didn't sleep well last night because of the wind and the tree outside my window tap, tap tapping on the windowpane."

"Did you speak to Sebastian or see him after his phone call to the police?" enquired Duchess Cassandra.

"No. No, I didn't. Why is there something wrong?"

"I think we should check on him. I'm going to the library." said Cassandra.

"W... wait for me." said a still sluggish Professor.

"And me." Ulysses and Ben called in unison.

They all trooped out of the drawing room to the library where they were met by a closed door. Knocking they waited but heard no response and no sound from within.

"He's probably gone for a walk or something." said the Professor hopefully.

Benjamin knocked once more then tried the door knob and found it locked. "What should we do?"

Ulysses suggested, "Try his study. It is next door and there is an adjoining door."

They all rushed to the study and entering found the adjoining door shut and locked.

"What now?"

"Call Jarvis. He must have a key." reasoned Duchess Cassandra. She stepped over to the ancient bell pull behind the desk and gave it a tug. Within moments Jarvis appeared silently in the doorway.

"May I be of some assistance, gentlemen, Duchess?" he enquired emotionlessly.

"We're concerned that something may have happened to your master. The last anyone saw him he was on his way to the library to make a phone call and now we find both doors locked and no response to our knocks. Do you have the key?" explained Cassandra, panic rising in her voice.

"Let me see if my old key still works." said Jarvis stepping up to the door between the library and the study.

"I'm afraid there is something blocking my key. It won't go in the lock."

"Step back and give me the key." demanded Benjamin. Attempting to insert the key he too found it blocked and handing the key back to Jarvis remarked, "He's right something's been wedged in the lock. Let's try the library hall door."

The little party filed to the library door where Jarvis once again tried his key but to no avail. "I'm afraid this lock has been jammed as well." said the butler, emotion ever so slightly rising in his voice.

Benjamin ran outside and around to the library windows. He could see the Earl slumped over a library table and what appeared to be blood pooling around his feet on the floor beneath. He tried the door but it was latched from the inside so removing his coat and wrapping it around his arm he used his elbow to break one of the small panes of glass in the door. Reaching in, he unlatched the door and hurriedly entered, rushing to Sebastian's side he checked for a pulse.

He could hear the alarmed beating of fists on the door. "All right, all right. I'm coming. Something terrible has happened. Sebastian has been murdered." Benjamin shouted. "Jarvis?"

"Yes, sir."

"Call the police immediately! The rest of you, we must preserve the crime scene, so no one is to enter this room. I will go back out the way I came in, through the patio door." directed Benjamin calmly.

6 ISI PAYS TRIBUTE

"Extortion turns a wise person into a fool, and a bribe corrupts the heart." -*Ecclesiastes 7:7*

Isidore Marion Boring whose real name was Isidore Abacas Beancounter had been a timid and delicate, only child growing up in a two bedroom council flat coddled by his deeply reserved parents. His family was of modest means with his dad a bookkeeper and his mum a knitter. His teachers and peers had thought him dull witted but still waters run deep, as they say. Isi read incessantly. He would hide himself away in his lonely room for hours on end only coming out for mealtimes and school. His preferred genre was fantasy and biographical accounts of the interests and lifestyles of the wealthy and of mountebanks[7].

Isi had not excelled scholastically but had an exceptionally active imagination. He had received his General Certificate of Secondary Education at age sixteen and then apprenticed under his father as a bookkeeper.

His old dad had been pushing him to go out, meet some young people his own age. His mum had been dropping hints about grandchildren. So, one

---

[7] a person who gains others confidence in order to cheat them

particularly lonesome Friday night he somehow found the courage to go to his local. Dressed in black polyester slacks, beige corduroy sports coat, smelling of dust and suede penny loafers, he splashed on eau de toilet and strolled to his local pub.

Nervously opening the door he was greeted by the smells of beer and stale tobacco and the raucous sounds of the usual Friday night crowd enjoying themselves. Once inside he ordered a shandy and tried to chat up women as they came to the bar for refreshments.

After several attempts at conversation he fannied around[8] nursing his shandy. He'd been sitting on his toddy[9] at the bar for about an hour when a bloke that had been dancing with several women sat on the stool next to him at the bar and ordered a pint of the pub's best bitter. He turned to Isi and remarked, "All right[10] mate? Why so glum chum? What a smashing night. The birds are plentiful and willing to knees up[11] all night. What more could a bloke ask for?"

"Cobblers[12]. Not for me. I'm nothing but a prat, an object of ridicule in their eyes. I've tried to chat with the young ladies and got nowt but rebuffs. I overheard two cheeky women laughing and referring to me as gormless and naff. I think it's time I went home." moaned a very dejected Isidore.

"Hard lines mate. Don't take it personal, like. It's just that you don't know the secret." Isi's new friend said with a sly wink.

"Oi, what're you trying to flog? What secret's that then?" whinged Isi sceptically but with the fascination of a drowning man.

"You just need a bit of bottle and a line, a story like, see? You need an edge, an advantage like. Create an air of mystery, a persona like and bingo bango bongo. Get it?" his new found mentor explained.

---

[8] procrastinate
[9] alone or on his own
[10] Hello. How are you?
[11] dance or party
[12] rubbish

"You mean tell porkies[13]?" Isi groused.

"It's all part of the game, innit? The birds like a little mystery and romance. They'll even help you by filling in the blanks if you play your cards right and don't give too many details, see. You just need to blag[14] it. Come outside with me, mate. Say, what's your name anyroad? My name's Gaylord Glick but the birds know me as Juan Fordarode, see."

"Isidore. My name's Isidore but people call me Isi." he said gloomily as he followed his mentor.

"Nice to meet you Isi. I'm going to reinvent you into a babe magnet. First we've got to give you a new moniker. How about, Mick Jaguar?"

"I like it Gaylord. What's next?"

"No, no call me Juan. Now turn up your coat collar and unbutton your shirt collar.

When we go back in you select a target and move around the room keeping to the shadows and approach your target from her blind spot. When you arrive step into her field of vision and say, 'You'd like to dance with me wouldn't you.'

When she replies, 'Why? Whatever do you mean?'

You respond, 'Quick, it's a matter of life and death.'

Then look around furtively then you say, 'My name is Jaguar... Mick Jaguar and I need your help. Our country needs your help'."

Isi was gobsmacked when his newly contrived persona was a resounding success. It was that night he experienced an epiphany and set his life on a path of personal discovery and adventure that few people are ever fortunate enough to enjoy.

His latest reincarnation as Doctor and Professor of Philosophy was a doddle compared to the complexities of his previous incarnations of Isi Gil Tiornot, Barrister; Dr. Les Moody, psychoanalyst; and Dr. Daryl B. Payne,

---

[13] lies
[14] bluff or wangle

surgeon. Even so, now he was playing for higher stakes, his life.

His little ploy had worked a treat as he had known it would. He had known from the moment he saw Ulysses' eyes glaze over that he would make a hasty exit leaving him alone. He was free to go about his affairs without being observed.

Not that what he had to do was enjoyable, far from it. He had been forking out a monthly ritual tribute ever since he had had the misfortune of bumping into one of his old surgery patients at a cocktail party. They had made quite a scene, praising his work and introducing him to their friends. Alas, Isi had morphed into the new persona of philosopher. One of the guests he was introduced to had been Sebastian Monk, the not so honourable, Earl of Uppington on the Downs.

He had come to a troublesome decision to end the bleeding once and for all. This would be his last payment.

7 WISDOM'S CALL

"Up the water and over the lea, that's the way for Billy and me"[15]

The scene was one of a perfect idyll. The azure sky was cloudless with just enough breeze to gently sail a kite. Two youngsters sat on the fiver bank fishing for tiddlers in the River Annan as it made its way happily through the town. Swans and geese drifted serenely among the lilies and punters poled flat bottomed boats ferrying their sweethearts lazily along the river past the pub where Logan, in fatigue tactical pursuit shorts and khaki ultra light short sleeve field shirt that hugged his ruggedly chiselled body, reclined idly on a blanket on lush well manicured lawns by the river bank.

He and Christine were from different worlds. He was of modest middle class background with a public school education, enlisted in the military at eighteen years of age and at nineteen years of age he was accepted into the SAS. After leaving the SAS he was recruited into the Kilmarnock Constabulary by his very good friend and mentor Superintendent Hamish Mac a' Phearsain or Mac. Her father a Marquis and her brother an Earl. She

---

[15] James Hogg (1770 - 1835), A Boy's Song

37

was independently wealthy and had attended Oxford with a first in Masters Criminology and Criminal Justice and then a PhD.

Were they chalk and cheese he wondered? Was their mutual penchant to help others and see justice done enough to create an enduring relationship? She was wise, funny and so beautiful.

He was deep in thought, when Christine interrupted with their picnic lunch. She said, "Penny for..."

Logan replied, "Oh, I was just thinking about my... uh... I mean, our future."

"Oh, do we have a future?" she playfully teased.

"I was just thinking how beautiful you are and how much I enjoy your company."

"Do go on." Lady Christine entreated.

But before he could get the next word out his phone began to buzz breaking the spell. "Oh, bollocks. Sorry, Cat, but I must take this.

Wisdom here" he responded irritably.

The voice on the other end was that of Commander Tiffany Raider. "I regret to intrude on your Sunday afternoon Detective Chief Inspector Wisdom but we have a situation. We may have a serial killer on our hands. I've sent everything we have to you to get you up to speed. The most recent, and possibly linked, incident took place at Monks Hall. Earl of Uppington on the Downs, Sebastian Monk, has been found murdered. You will need to get onto the local Bobbies, coroner and check with the forensics as soon as possible."

"I'll get on it right away, Commander." said a frustrated Logan.

"I'm counting on you, DCI Wisdom, to handle this not only expeditiously but with your utmost discretion." and with that Raider hung up.

"This has been a wonderful day Cat but duty calls. I'll drop you at Lochwood Hall, shall I?" he offered as he began gathering up the picnic bits and pieces.

Cat's curiosity was getting the better of her. "It has been a brilliant day, Logan. When will I see you again?"

"I can't say. I don't know quite what I'm in for on this one, Cat. I'm off to Toadspool in the Dell. There's been a death at Monks Hall." he confided seriously.

"Who was it? Surely not Sebastian Monk? Whatever happened? Was it a shooting accident?" blurted out Lady Christine.

"Ah, curiosity killed the cat, Christine." said Logan with a wry grin.

"Yes but, satisfaction brought it back, my dear Logan. So, what can you tell me?" Christine pressed.

"It was, in fact, Sebastian Monk, Earl of Uppington on the Downs. It appears he was garrotted. We're awaiting the coroner's findings. The local plods have been trampling all over the crime scene and Forensics is there as we speak and I've got to hop to it." Logan replied as they walked to his pride and joy, his 1985 British racing green 4 X 4 Range Rover Vogue.

"Oh no! How horrible!" exclaimed Cat.

"Sebastian and I have known each other since childhood. Bartholomew and I spent time each summer holiday in the Lake District at Monks Hall and Sebastian would visit Lochwood Hall each summer. I will have to call on his mother to offer my condolences.

I know Sebastian's social standing would necessitate a senior officer's presence but surely the local police have a higher-ranking officer that could provide the appearance of venerated supervision. What is there about this case that would require a senior officer of the Metropolitan Police to be in attendance?" queried Lady Christine with concern creeping into her voice.

"I can't give you a clear answer because I'm not up to speed yet but it seems that there have been other deaths that may or may not be connected in some way. More than one jurisdiction may be involved as a result the Yard has been assigned the task.

I'm sure it's been blown out of proportion and I'll give you a call as soon as I'm finished and we can pick up where we left off." Logan said affectionately as he tentatively put his arm around Christine.

Christine smiled warmly as they reached the Vogue and Logan opened the door for her. They drove in companionable silence back to Lochwood Hall. Alighting from the car Christine turned to Logan and leaning close kissed him tenderly on the cheek.

Logan wore a silly grin and he couldn't feel the ground beneath his feet as he took the few steps back to his car.

He beamed foolishly from ear to ear all the way to Toadspool in the Dell, Cumbria.

Stepping from the car at Monks Hall, in a dark blue Hugo Boss suit, he was greeted by Sergeant B. Goodman, a veritable mountain of a man with sandy hair and friendly blue eyes. "State your business here, sir." the Sergeant demanded in his booming bass voice.

"Good afternoon, Sergeant. I'm D.C.I. Wisdom from the Met."

"Oh, beg pardon, Guv'nor. I've been expecting you, sir. Sergeant B. Goodman at your disposal."

"Time of death Sergeant?"

Sergeant Goodman checked his notes, "Umm, the nearest the Coroner would place the time of death until she had a chance to examine the body in her lab was between 11:00 and 16:00 hours sir."

"Cause of death?"

The Sergeant again referred to his notes, "Garrotte, Guv'nor. The Doc said that all she can tell us now is that there was a combined affect from the ligature but she will be able to give a more accurate answer after she gets 'im on 'er table."

"Right. Can you show me where the Earl's body was found?"

"Right this way, Guv. The forensics team has finished and the Coroner is waiting for your release of the body, sir."

"Thank you, Sergeant. Has anything been disturbed?" he asked as he donned the blue shoe coverings and latex gloves.

"Only the forensics team and Coroner have been on the scene, Guv. Oh, and a Mr. Benjamin Wolf who discovered the body, sir."

"Have all of the guests and staff been detained for questioning?"

"Yes Guv. My men are taking their statements now."

"I would like to speak to Mr. Wolf as soon as I'm finished here."

"Yes sir, Guv."

"Please wait out here Sergeant and see that I'm not disturbed." Logan took a step inside the patio doors and stopped, carefully scrutinizing every minute detail of the scene.

"Oh, Sergeant."

"Yes Guv?"

Logan noticed that the Earl's hand was still resting on the telephone. "Have phone records been checked to determine if the Earl had recently made a call?"

"No Guv but I'll get someone on it right away."

Logan went through the pockets of the dead man, a procedure he always felt uneasy performing as if it was an affront to the deceased. He removed from the Earl's rich burgundy, Melton wool waistcoat watch pocket a small key that the forensics team had missed. Examining the key he spotted a symbol he didn't recognize and a number. He found nothing further in the man's pockets. Placing the key in an evidence bag he called to the Sergeant, "You can let the Coroner know I'm finished with the body."

"Right you are, Guv'nor."

Logan noted that from the position of the body and the fact he was garrotted from behind that the Earl must have known and been comfortable enough with his assailant to have allowed him or her to cross behind him.

He next checked the door leading to the foyer and then the adjoining door to the Earl's study and found them both to be locked with something jammed into each of the locks preventing insertion of a key. He also noted that the glass of one of the windowpanes in the patio door had been broken inward, the shards of broken window glass still on the carpet.

"Were all of the doors into the library found locked?"

"The witnesses all reported finding them locked and something lodged in the hall and library door locks preventing them from getting a key in. Mr. Wolf had to break the glass in the patio door in order to open the latch." reported Sergeant Goodman.

"Hmm, I see." said Logan as he left the library and headed for the study. On his way he checked the foyer library door and finding it both locked and the lock blocked he continued on to the study. Once again he took only a single step inside the door and then stood still, slowly surveying the room. When he was satisfied he approached the desk and carefully inspected all of the items there. Finally, he perused the Earl's personal planner and several puzzling entries caught his attention, Friday: 10:00 (1) CK; Saturday: 10:00 (2) LK; 11:00 (3) DK; 13:00 (4) CK; 15:00 (5) LK; Sunday: 11:30 (M) X.

It seems that the Earl had his own code and Logan thought it could be important. He looked through the entire planner but could not find a solution to the code. He searched through the desk with no success. He decided the code would have to wait and checked the door adjoining the library. It too was locked and the lock blocked. He needed to talk to the butler.

Just then Sergeant Goodman entered the study, "I'm going to begin my interviews. Would you please have the butler, what was his name, come to the study?"

"Jarvis, sir, that's his name. I'll fetch him immediately, Guv."

"Thank you Sergeant."

Before Sergeant Goodman could turn around Jarvis appeared beside him making the Sergeant jump. "Blimey!" he exclaimed.

"Come in Jarvis. I'm D.C.I. Logan Wisdom and I'm here to investigate the death of your employer, Sebastian Monk. I just want to clear up a few things. I understand you were summoned to unlock the two doors leading into the library, is that correct?"

"Yes sir."

"What time was this and where were you at the time?"

"It was precisely eleven minutes past four o'clock when I was summoned. I was in the wine cellar selecting the wine for the evening meal." responded Jarvis.

"And did you notice anything unusual about any of the guests when you arrived in the main foyer?"

Jarvis paused considering his answer, "No sir...but..."

"Yes, Jarvis? Even the most insignificant incongruity might be vitally important."

"Well, sir. It's just that, Mr. Upman didn't seem bothered. It was more as though he was impatient than concerned. He kept looking at his empty glass."

"I see. How many keys are there to the library and where are they kept?"

"There are just the two keys, sir. I have one and the Earl has the other." replied the butler.

"Where did the Earl keep his key?"

"He kept in his pocket, sir."

"Let me have your key to the library doors, Jarvis."

"Very good sir. There you are sir." the butler dutifully handed the key to the D.C.I.

"Thank you Jarvis that will be all for now. You've been a great help. Please tell the Sergeant I'd like to see him, as you leave."

Sergeant Goodman entered the room looking expectant, "Yes, Guv? You wanted to see me?"

"Yes Sergeant. Did forensics find any keys on or around the body?"

"Yes, Guv. Would you like me to fetch them?"

"Yes, bring all of the Earl's personal effects in here and put them on the desk and while you're about it have Jarvis bring us a cuppa, will you? Then you can send Mr. Benjamin Wolf in, please."

"Yes, Guv."

Logan examined the Earl's effects and finding a set of keys he compared the key Jarvis had given him with all of them and found the matching key. Logan muttered to himself, "So, how did the killer commit the murder, lock the doors and block the locks escaping with the doors still locked without a key?"

Benjamin Wolf had entered the room unobserved overhearing the D.C.I.'s musings. "Sounds as if you might be looking for an Illusionist, D.C.I. Wisdom."

"Yes... yes perhaps I am." Logan said thoughtfully.

"You wanted to see me, D.C.I. Wisdom?"

"Indeed I did, Mr. Wolf. I just had a few points that I needed to clear up.

What was your relationship to the deceased?"

"We've been friends for years."

"I understand you were on a walking holiday. Is that correct?"

"Yes."

"What was your walking tour itinerary, Mr. Wolf?"

"I set out from my cottage in Keswick Thursday morning around 7:00 a.m. and walked about eighteen miles the first day to Penrith following the old railway line. I spent the night in the Bide-A-While Bed and Breakfast in Penrith. Friday I walked about thirteen glorious miles from Penrith to Glenridding on Ullswater and enjoyed a delicious meal at the Hide-A-Way Bed and Breakfast and set out Saturday morning for the final leg of my journey to Monks Hall, Toadspool in the Dell.

I found the village a rather bleak place I'm afraid. I did notice something I thought was out of place but it was probably nothing. Just eerie stillness stimulating my imagination I suspect."

"Oh, and what was that then?" Logan's attention alerted. It was anomalies that any good detective looked for.

"I noticed a shiny new Z 200 Roadster parked down a side street and I thought I saw someone trying to hide from view."

The DCI's interest was instantly peeked, "Were you aware, Mr. Wolf, that that fits with the description of the missing woman's motor? Did you, by any chance, know the missing woman, Mr. Wolf?"

Ben responded reluctantly, "I knew of her, DCI Wisdom. I met her mother, Brandy D. Canter, many years ago when I was just entering college. Chrystal was in the hospital at the time."

"I see. And you haven't been in contact with Chrystal or her mother through the years?"

"Sadly, no. I had no idea how to get in touch and by the time I was ready I was sure it was too late."

"We'll leave that for the moment.

So your route took you through Rolling Downs about what, lunch time, Friday?" queried Logan.

"Yes, I arrived at about 12:45. I stopped at The Stone the Crows Pub, ordered a ploughman and washed it down with a pint of scrumpy.

Look D.C.I. Wisdom, I know what you're implying and I did not murder Picov Andropov." Ben responded disdainfully.

"I'm not accusing you of anything, Mr. Wolf. I'm simply trying to create a timeline of everyone's movements for the times in question.

Now, if you wouldn't mind telling me what your connection was to Mr. Andropov?" Logan asked sternly.

"He was an acquaintance, nothing more."

"When did you last see the Earl?"

"It was gone one o'clock. He had just had a lecture from Duchess Cassandra on his moral obligation to tell the constabulary everything he knew about Chrystal D. Canter. He had decided that perhaps she had a point and he went off to call the local plod to impart a rumour concerning Miss Canter and a married man."

"I see. And what did you do then, Mr. Wolf?"

"Professor Boring, an entirely apt name I must say, began to haver philosophical on the subject of money, of all things. I poured myself pint of Guinness and went for a stroll. I found myself a quiet seat in the garden and read a wonderful mystery by Martha Grimes."

"What time did you return to the drawing room and what time did you decide to look for the Earl?"

"It was gone four o'clock and time for a cocktail when we all met in the drawing room and, I suppose, it was about twenty past four when Duchess Cassandra became concerned."

"I believe you were the first one to reach the library door. Is that correct?"

"Yes, yes. I guess I was. I found the door in the hall locked so someone, I think it was that real estate fellow, suggested trying the adjoining door in the study. It was locked as well. Someone rang for Jarvis and he tried his keys but both locks were blocked with something and he couldn't get his key in. So, I rushed outside to try the French doors from the veranda and found them locked. I knew something was wrong when I saw Sebastian slumped over the desk so I broke the windowpane and let myself in.

There was a lot of blood. I checked for a pulse and shouted for someone to call the police. And here we are."

"Did you happen to notice the time you found the Earl? Did you touch anything or move anything?"

"I was a little preoccupied to notice the time, Detective Chief Inspector. No, to my knowledge I didn't touch anything other than trying to find a pulse and, of course, the door to get in. Everyone was pounding on the study door to be let in but I told them no one must enter until the police have been."

"How very judicious of you, Mr. Wolf. Did you notice anything out of place or unusual?"

"You mean other than my friend dead with his throat cut? No. I wasn't really thinking about that sort of thing at the time, was I?" Benjamin came back with acerbically.

"Well, if you think of anything, sir, please let me know. It may be important in helping find who did this to your friend."

"Yes, yes. I'm sorry Detective Chief Inspector."

"Thank you for your cooperation, Mr. Wolf.

What is it that you do for a living, Mr. Wolf?"

"I'm a consultant. I instruct those predisposed on safe, secure techniques of protecting things and themselves."

"How very interesting if not somewhat woolly. That will be all for now, Mr. Wolf but I'm afraid I'll have to ask you remain at Monks Hall for the time being."

Benjamin turned to leave but before he got to the door D.C.I. Wisdom called out, "Oh, one more thing, Mr. Wolf. How did you know the key holes were blocked?"

"Jarvis tried inserting his key and told us the holes were blocked. I took the key from Jarvis and I too tried the key in the lock and found it to be blocked."

"Thank you, Mr. Wolf."

"Will that be all, D.C.I. Wisdom?"

"Yes, thank you, Mr. Wolf. You may go."

Logan directed the Sergeant to fetch Duchess Cassandra for her interview.

A few minutes later the enchanting Duchess Cassandra languidly drifted into the study with an air of elegance and sophistication. She was one of those women that with one smouldering glance had the awesome ability to chew you up and spit you out and you'd simply be thankful she noticed you. "You summoned me, Detective?"

D.C.I. Logan's rugged six foot two muscular frame, jet black hair and steely blue eyes had not gone unnoticed.

"Detective Chief Inspector Logan Wisdom, Duchess Cassandra." he reproved. "Yes, I need your help to clear up a few points.

Now then, Duchess Cassandra what were your movements between one o'clock and the time the Earl's body was discovered?"

"Cassandra, please, Logan. May I call you Logan?"

"It is D.C.I. Wisdom, Duchess Cassandra."

Duchess Cassandra was clearly taken aback by her apparent lack of effect on D.C.I. Wisdom.

"Very well, D.C.I. Wisdom, I went for a walk with Ulysses Upman. We hadn't gotten very far before he rudely took a business call which seemed to go on forever so I left him to it and continued to stroll the gardens."

"Where did your stroll take you?"

"Well, I don't know if I should be embarrassed or not but I went in search of an apparition I witnessed during the storm." she divulged somewhat sheepishly.

"What was it that you thought you saw?" asked Logan curiously.

Duchess Cassandra was wishing she hadn't spoken so candidly, "During the height of the storm in a brilliant flash of lightening I thought I saw a man standing at the edge of the forest half turned toward the house with... Now you are going to think I'm crazy but I thought I saw a huge wolf by his side."

"Did you find any evidence of your apparition?" said Logan calmly.

"No. No, I didn't." she replied somewhat crestfallen.

"Did anyone see you or did you see anyone that could confirm your whereabouts?"

"No. No one saw me and I saw no one until I met Mr. Upman just returning to the house and we went in together."

"What time was this, Duchess Cassandra?"

"It must have just gone four because Ben, I mean, Mr. Wolf, was offering everyone cocktails. I remember thinking it was strange that our host hadn't joined us so I asked if anyone had seen Sebastian. That's when I decided to look for him."

"Where was Professor I. M. Boring during all of this, Duchess

Cassandra?"

"He was evidently dozing on a settee in front of the window. He came to when he heard his name mentioned.?"

"Had no one noticed him laying there?"

"No. The sofa is turned toward the window so unless one stepped up to the window in front of the settee they would not see anyone laying there."

"I see." said Logan. "One more thing. Why were you all here? I mean, it seemed an odd combination of guests."

"Sebastian could seem eccentric at times and he thought that quirky groupings made social gatherings more interesting.

Will that be all Detective Chief Inspector? I'm developing a headache and need a couple of paracetamol. I could use something bracing to wash them down will you join me Detective Chief Inspector?" Duchess Cassandra entreated in her most beguiling manner.

"No, thank you, Duchess Cassandra. We're through here but keep yourself available in case I need to question you further.

Please ask Sergeant Goodman to come in on your way out." and with that the Duchess turned on her heel and stalked out of the study stopping briefly to speak to the Sergeant.

Sergeant Goodman entered the study asking, "Yes, Guv? You wanted to see me?"

"Yes, Sergeant. Send in Mr. Ulysses Upman, please. And then, do you think you could rustle up a sandwich and another cuppa. I missed my tea and I could eat a horse and chase the rider."

"Yes, Guv. I'm sure cook will put something together for you."

A few minutes later and Logan was joined by Ulysses Upman. "Good evening Mr. Upman. I'm D.C.I. Logan Wisdom. I have one or two questions to put to you.

What was your relationship with the deceased?"

"I manage the Earl's portfolio of international real estate holdings. We met ten years ago at a seminar on American real estate investing at Harvard and our association developed from there."

"What happens to his real estate portfolio after his death?"

"His son, Viscount Charles Monk, will take over everything, including the real estate portfolio. Chip has been managing the portfolio for some time. I am only called upon as an advisor. As a point of fact he will not receive further benefit beyond that which he is already enjoying, D.C.I. Wisdom."

"I see and where might I find Viscount Charles Monk?"

"He lives in London. I can get you his contact details. However, as it happens, he is due to visit with his grandmother, Countess Vera Lee Isay Monk tomorrow. She makes her home in the east wing."

"Has she been notified of her son's death?"

"Yes, she has and has not taken the news very well, I'm afraid. The doctor has given her something to sedate her and she is resting in her bed. The Countess is ninety years of age and very frail, indeed, Detective Chief Inspector."

"I see and where did you go after Duchess Cassandra left you?"

"I had a business call that I had to take and I was on it for some time and when I finished Cass..., uh, Duchess Cassandra was nowhere to be found so I strolled through the conservatory admiring some of the rare species Sebastian has been able to acquire and then I made my way back to the drawing room meeting the Duchess on the way."

"Can anyone confirm your whereabouts?"

"I'm afraid I was alone most of the time not realizing I was going to need an alibi. You could check my phone records or you can speak with my alternative fuel analyst, Amanda Livering Cole. I'm negotiating a wind farm. You could also speak with my accounts payable administrator, Imelda Czechs. She called me in a flap about one of my accounts. They can corroborate my time on the phone but I'm afraid I was alone after that."

DCI Wisdom made a note and dismissed Ulysses Upman with, "Thank you Mr. Upman. That's all I need for the present but for now please do not leave Monks Hall I might need to speak with you again.

Please tell the Sergeant I would like to see him on your way out."

Sergeant B. Goodman anticipated his superior's requirement. Opening the study door he ushered in the Professor announcing with a smile, "Last one Guv.

Cook made you a sandwich of sweet Italian sausage fried until it's crisp and brown with sliced red, yellow and green peppers cooked in the fat along with some sliced onion in a fresh Italian roll and a steaming cuppa. She hopes you enjoy it, Guv." he said placing the gastronomic tour de force in front of D.C.I. Wisdom.

"Thank you Sergeant, you're a life saver and thank cook for me will you." he said handing the Sergeant a note and taking a huge bite of the culinary masterpiece.

Turning to the Professor he introduced himself, "Professor Boring I am D.C.I. Logan Wisdom of the Metropolitan Police Force and I need to ask you some questions. It's getting late so I'll be as brief as possible.

How did you know the Earl?"

"Sebastian, uh... that is... The Earl attended one of my lectures. It seems uh seemed that he had a keen interest in philosophy. I was introduced to him after my lecture and we had dinner together that evening. He thought I might be able to... I don't know... add something to the conversation I suppose."

"I see and where were you between one o'clock and the time the Earl's body was discovered?"

"I tried to engage Mr. Wolf in a conversation on the meaning and purpose of currency but he seemed uninterested and rudely quoted scripture to me then poured himself a drink and left in a huff. I don't know what I did to provoke his response I'm sure. Words have both a literal meaning and emotional impact you know."

"What time did Mr. Wolf part company with you?"

"Oh, the others had left the room by that time. I'd say about five or six minutes after one o'clock and my exchange with Mr. Wolf, such as it was, lasted only about three or four minutes."

"What did you do after that?"

"I tried to read an article in The Philosophers' Quarterly on the subject of I Don't Need Anger Management: I need people to stop cheesing me off. by Theloneliest Mediocrities but the sunshine streaming in the window made me sleepy and I dozed off. I hadn't slept well the night before and, I guess, I didn't realize just how tired I was.

I must have slept soundly because the next thing I remember was hearing my name mentioned."

"I take it no one can confirm that you didn't leave the drawing room between the hours of one o'clock and four o'clock?"

"I'm afraid that is correct, Detective Chief Inspector."

"That will be all for now, Professor Boring but keep yourself available for further questions." Logan said wearily.

He dismissed the Sergeant, who seemed fit to drop, "I'm knackered and you must be too. Go home to your wife and kiddies, Sergeant. Get some rest and I'll see you back here at 08:00 on the dot to go over what we've been able to glean so far.

Good night Sergeant."

"Good night, Guv'nor."

8 BEYOND GOOD & EVIL

"Do not be overcome by evil, but overcome evil with good." - Romans 12:21 ESV

Moonlight streamed in through the bedroom window and stars twinkled in the blue black night sky. All around her were unnerving sounds of the old house creaking and groaning as it settled for the night. A barn owl screeched sounding like that of a blood curdling woman's scream. Suddenly she was startled by a scraping at her window pane whilst a terrifyingly menacing black shadow crept slowly across her room. Just when the ghostly hands were about to reach over the comforter she turned her head and noticed the branch of a tree next to the house was the evil culprit.

Duchess Cassandra lay staring at the ceiling with her comforter pulled up to her chin listening to all of the night sounds. Some she could explain away and others defied explanation.

Unexpectedly she was back in the bedroom she had shared with her sister, Cornett. It was as real as if it was happening at that very moment. She was paralyzed but she sensed something evil was lurking. Then she heard it. The awful frenzied beating, the piercing wailing of a young girl and the angry shrill yelling of a mother trying to defend her child. Then the evil fiend turned his cruel attention on her mother letting the child go free. Chrystal watched in fascinated horror as Cornett came running into their bedroom and hid under their bed. The expression on her sister's face made her blood run cold. It was the emotionless look of an executioner.

The tyrant finally tired of his violent onslaught and ceased his malicious attack on Brandy, their mother. Listening, she could hear the soul wrenching sobs of their mother and growling bellow of Sebastian Monk as he strode angrily down the stairs.

Then she was in the playroom of a hospital. She could smell disinfectant, and medicine and hear the nurses bustling about from room to room. This time it was her sister's turn to be repaired like a broken delicate porcelain doll. Her mother appeared in the doorway, battered and bruised, saying, "Come Chrystal. It's time to go now. Your sister's out of surgery and will be fine." Then waking with a start she found herself drenched in perspiration and shaking.

Chrystal had suffered her share of beatings but they did not seem to have left her as mentally scarred as her sister. Cornett never smiled after her last stay in hospital.

She lay motionless thinking about her life. After they had escaped the cruelty of their mother's first husband and their father they had fled to Spain. Following a very hostile divorce their mother met Alvaro Canter and fell deeply in love. It wasn't long before Brandy and Alvaro were wed. He made a wonderful, caring husband to Brandy and father to the girls.

It was only a few short years when tragedy struck the happy little family. Alvaro was found floating face down in one of the winery vats. Forensics determined he had high levels of tropane alkaloids found in the plant, devil's trumpet. The preponderance of circumstantial evidence seemed to lead straight to Brandy. Shortly afterwards Brandy mysteriously disappeared, never to be found, fuelling the fire of rumour and innuendo. Fortunately, by this time, the girls had grown into beautiful young women about to embark on new adventures.

Cornett had read Botany at the University of Cambridge achieving a PhD in Plant Sciences and her PhD in Naturopathic Medicine from the National

University of Natural Medicine.

While reading English Literature at the University of Oxford she had met the Duke Clarence Oliver Bradley (C.O.B.) Webb, Duke of Camelot and Chief Executive Officer of Venitia, a global precision luxury automobile manufacturer. She could still remember the day they met. She had just entered the Oxford University Fencing Club for practice where a handsome young man and his friends were having a natter. She overheard him bragging about his swordplay skills in a vain attempt to impress several young ladies.

Chrystal slipped into the dressing room to put on her fencing kit before going into the gym to practice. She took up a position in front of the mirrors to practice lunges, one of the foundation moves in fencing. Watching the mirrors for any problems with her form. Next she selected smallest target ball, a one inch rubber ball to practice sword control then she continued by standing a sword's length away from a small disc on the wall and drawing circles around it with the sword tip. After that she worked on her footwork by a sequence of advance, advance lunge, on guard. Then she tried a jump forward lunge, redouble, on guard. To improve her parries she placed a block behind her back foot to remind her she could not step backward. Then she practiced an entirely offensive sequence where she was unable to retreat.

All the while the young man had been watching her. He couldn't take his eyes from her. Her enchanting beauty took his breath away. Her long, lustrous auburn hair framed her flawless ivory skin, dazzling emerald eyes, so deep a man could get lost in them and full lips. She moved her lithe physique with elegance and effortless efficiency of motion.

He moved closer and offered a few pointers on foot placement. It was at that moment their eyes met and her heart skipped a beat as she gazed upon the most classically masculine man she had ever met. A full and wavy head of dark hair crowned his chiselled countenance accentuated by prominent eye brows over smouldering eyes and a strong jaw. He possessed a charismatic self-confident air, in short he was an Adonis.

She turned her face up to his saying, "Excuse me but I couldn't help overhear your conversation. I would love the opportunity to fence with you."

He rose to the challenge eager to show off his superior swordplay skills.

Whereupon she set to work soundly thrashing her Adonis at which a round of giggles could be heard emanating from a few of his female admirers.

Afterward he had introduced himself, "I'm afraid we haven't been properly introduced. I am Clarence O. B. Webb, Duke of Camelot at your service. You may call me Cob." He waited expectantly for her to reciprocate.

"Cor, pull the other one." she said with disbelief.

Chuckling, the Duke reached in his kit bag and withdrew his wallet opening his wallet he revealed his identification and pointed to his family crest emblazoned on his tunic.

As realization began to set in she felt her face begin to redden. She curtsied and apologized profusely to which he said, "I think that makes us even. Would you please do me the honour of joining me for dinner? I'll pick you up, say sevenish this evening?"

"I...I d... don't know what to say."

"That's easy. Say yes."

"Y... yes."

Love blossomed and within a year Cob popped the question. It was a perfect July day in Oxford. The golden sun shone high in the sky with a few scattered cotton baton clouds floating serenely in a pale blue sky. A gentle breeze stirred tiny wavelets on the River Isis as punts glided tranquilly to and fro carrying their courting couples and trumpeter swans moved gracefully upon the water in a sublime idyll.

Chrystal sat lethargically taking in the pastoral scene peacefully enjoying the gentle breeze while she waited for Cob to return from the nearby pub with their drinks and sandwiches. All of a sudden Cob was kneeling in front of her on one knee clothed in a Royal Duke's robe of the best handmade silk velvet trimmed with the finest Canadian ermine. He wore a silver-gilt circlet with eight strawberry leaves.

It was like living in a fairytale. Chrystal laughed until she noticed his outstretched hand holding a spectacular platinum ring set with a full carat oval cut emerald of the most intensely pure green not equalled by anything else in nature. A double halo of diamonds curved gently around the exquisite emerald and continued in a pavé setting along the band.

"Love bears all things, believes all things, hopes all things, endures all things. Love never fails.

Chrystal D. Canter, I vow to help you love life, to always hold you with tenderness and to have the patience that love demands, to speak when words are needed and to share the silence when they are not and to live within the warmth of your heart now and forever. Will you be my wife accepting this ring signifying my undying love?"

Chrystal had stopped laughing and began to cry with joy as she tearfully accepted.

After the wedding Chrystal D. Canter became known as Her Grace Cassandra Webb, Duchess of Camelot.

9 CAT & CHIP

"I wandered lonely as a cloud[16]"

Lady Christine had packed an overnight case and set out in her 1967, vintage Austin-Healey, Mark III, 3000, Healey metallic blue with walnut veneer dash, buttery soft hand stitched leather upholstery that fit her like a custom made glove and 150 hp, twin carburettor engine. She stopped briefly at the local florist to pick up an appropriate bouquet of flowers before she turned her motor towards Toadspool in the Dell.

Cat had called her aunt with her condolences. After a brief telephone reunion with the Viscount, Charles (Chip) Monk, she was invited to visit for a few days to help console the Countess. She was, of course, more than pleased to be of help in this time of crisis. The fact that the visit might assuage her passion for solving mysteries wouldn't go amiss either with the added bonus of being able to see Logan.

It was a glorious day for a drive. Cat began to sing as she drove. Her

---

ng line from Daffodils by William Wordsworth

hauntingly melodic voice seemed to float on the wind as she flew along the motorways, dual carriage ways and country lanes with the hood down and the wind running its fingers through her silky, jet black tresses.

She decided to take the scenic route, the A592 through the Lake District making a slight detour to stop for a picnic lunch at Aira[17] Force falls. The main force drops seventy feet from beneath a stone foot bridge providing a glimpse of a magnificently landscaped Victoria park with a dramatic scene of waterfalls, arboretum and rocky outcrops.

The Lake Poet, William Wordsworth frequented the locale of the Aira Force and was probably inspired to pen his poem, "Daffodils" as he observed daffodils growing on the Ullswater shore near the mouth of the Aira Beck[18].

The poet mentioned the Aira Force in three of his poems, the most famous of which is "The Somnambulist" where he writes in the final verse,

Wild stream of Aira, hold thy course,

Nor fear memorial lays,

Where clouds that spread in solemn shade,

Are edged with golden rays!

Dear art thou to the light of heaven,

Though minister of sorrow;

Sweet is thy voice at pensive even.

And thou, lovers' hearts forgiven,

Shalt take thy place with Yarrow.

Cat sat in the shade of an ancient and majestic English yew tree tucking into savoury and sweet treats from her hamper. The drive and fresh air had amplified her appetite. She delighted in an egg and cress sandwich washing it down with a flask of Pimm's and lemonade and for afters a custard tart and tea. Sufficiently fortified she gathered up her picnic bits and pieces and

---

[17] The river name Aira is derived from old Norse eyrr meaning gravel bank and old Norse á meaning a river, hence the river at gravel bank

[18] A brook, especially a swift running stream with steep banks

slipping into the Mark III like a well made racing glove Cat set out on the final leg of her journey.

Her thoughts, stirred by his remark about their future, turned to Logan and their relationship. In the beginning it had been the thrill of the pursuit but as she had come to know him she began to appreciate his unselfish generosity of spirit, cool logic, gallantry in the face of adversity and she could get lost in his steel blue eyes. She smiled as she thought about his way with children.

The miles flew by like flashing guardrail posts until at last she turned her roadster in at the gate to Monks Hall. Bringing the Mark III to a stop in front of the entrance to the Countess' apartment in the east wing she separated herself from the embrace of the blissfully comfy bucket seat just in time to be greeted by the Viscount, Chip Monk. "Hello my dear Christine." Chip gushed in the most toffee nosed manner Christine almost let out a guffaw until he kissed her. That was just too much and Lady Christine almost said and did something very unladylike but mustering all her fortitude she managed to wriggle out from his clutches and respond, "Hello Chip. How is Auntie Vera Lee?"

Viscount Charles Monk was a tall reedy man with a sallow complexion, greased back bleached blond hair and well manicured nails. He smelled of Turkish cigarettes and Clive Christian No. 1 Pure Perfume, a very floral fragrance on the feminine side of unisex, at US$2,350 or £1,636 for 30 millilitres or 1 ounce. Cat's finely tuned sense of smell was able to discern an enigmatic lemony bergamot[19] leading immediately into a jasmine floral blend of rose, carnation, lily of the valley, heliotrope with a hint of ylang. The base is that of sandalwood, patchouli, cedar, Tonka bean, vanilla, and a hint of cinnamon.

Lady Christine opened the boot retrieving her luggage.

"Oh, she's just as mulish as always but resting comfortably and anxious for your arrival. I'll take you to your room so you can freshen up before you visit her in her rooms. We can meet in the sitting room, after your visit, for drinks

---

[19] Citrus bergamia or bergamot orange is a fragrant fruit the size of an orange with a yellow colour similar to a lemon. Easily combined with an array of scents its scent is fruity-sweet with a mild spicy note.

before dinner." He said with a smarmy smirk and lead the way into the house without offering to take her overnight case.

Christine was swept back to her childhood as she entered Monks Hall. Images of playing games of hide and seek, skipping, five stones[20], and Oranges and Lemons[21] with Molly, Dot and Timmy Murphy, children of the butler and cook. Chip wasn't happy unless he could find a way to disrupt the game or inflict pain. He liked conkers where he would always purposely hit your knuckles and swear blind it was an accident. He was always pressurizing Timmy into malicious schemes and then laying all of the blame at Timmy's feet avowing innocence.

She was filled with annoyance as she recalled Chip tying jumping jacks to the cat's tail and laughing maniacally as poor Fluffy ran frantically this way and that trying to get away.

She was brought back to reality by the Viscount's rebuke, "Cat, you haven't been listening to a word I've said, have you? I was hoping I would find, in you, an ally. Grandmamma won't listen to reason.

Well, this is your room." Stepping aside so that she could enter he went on in his slimy manner, "We can continue our little tête-à-tête after dinner over a few drinks, Cat."

Lady Christine did not wish to endure any further exchange with the Viscount now or in the future and upon entering her room quickly closed the door in his face.

---

[20] This game used to play with small rounded stones but today we play it with plastic or metal jacks. The first player starts by throwing five stones or five jacks on the ground then taking the ball throws it in the air picking up one stone or one jack and then catches the ball before it hits the ground. Continuing until all the stones or jacks have been picked up.

[21] Based around an old English children's song Oranges and Lemons, about the sounds of church bells in various parts of London. Two children form an arch with their arms after secretly deciding which one is the orange and which the lemon, then everyone sings the song. The other children file through the arch until the song ends and the two children bring their arms down catching someone. The one caught is secretly asked if they are an orange or a lemon and then they are lined up behind the original player that is the orange or lemon.

After unpacking and freshening up Cat made her way to Countess Vera Lee Isay Monk's chambers and knocked tentatively on her door. The Countess' nurse, Barb Bituwitz, opened the door saying, "May I help you?"

Peering over the nurse's shoulder she beheld what could only be described as a time capsule. A young boy's portrait, that could only be that of Viscount Charles Monk, by Leonard Boden[22], a celebrated portrait artist, enshrined in a small alcove, showcased against a neutral wall with millwork that echoes the edges of the frame. The furnishings were that of a pair of Louis XVI wing back chairs, a pair of fauteuils[23] all upholstered in royal blue floral patterned fabric, and walnut coffee table. The blues and golds of the furnishings compliment the hand stencilled, striated Damask pattern of the sitting room walls enhanced by oyster silk curtains with coral and pale blue embellishments. Even the tassels and tiebacks were custom matched to the distinctive blue of the painting. Over the marble fireplace hung a landscape by John Constable. The room smelt of tea, camphor and memories.

"I'm Lady Christine..." but before she could finish the Countess heard her voice and called out, "Oh my, Christine, come in, come in, my dear. Get out of the doorway you silly goose and let Lady Christine pass. Don't stand there gawping I have perfectly good hearing and I'd know the sound of my favourite niece's voice anywhere. Now, go fetch us some tea and biscuits and be quick about it." ordered the Countess.

The tiny dowager lady sitting ramrod straight in her antique wheel chair was frail with snow white hair pulled tightly in a bun and adorned in mourning black lace and satin. Her bright, twinkling eyes surveyed Lady Christine affectionately and oddly enquiringly from behind wire rimmed spectacles.

Crossing the room to her aunt Lady Christine leaned down and gave her aunt a hug and a kiss on the cheek. Then, stepping over to the widow she asked, "It's very dark in here, Auntie, would you like me to open the drapes?"

---

[22] Leonard Monro Boden (Scotland 31 May 1911 - 15 November 1999) 19 portraits of members of British Royal family and favorite of Queen Elizabeth
[23] A style of open armed chair with a primarily exposed wooden frame originating in France in the early 17th century.

"No! No, please don't open them." pleaded her aunt anxiously.

Lady Christine regarded her aunt and dear family friend with fondness noticing a tear slowly trickle down her cheek. Rushing to her side Christine entreated, "Whatever is the matter Aunt Vera?"

"I'm just so happy to see you, Cat. Thank you so much for coming, my dear. Lately..." suddenly the bedroom door opened and the nurse entered the room carrying the tea tray.

"Would you like me to pour M' Lady?" asked the nurse.

"No, thank you, nurse. Lady Christine will play mother. Please leave us alone." instructed the Countess.

"Are you in some sort of trouble Aunt Vera?" Christine enquired anxiously.

"Oh Cat, I don't know." she replied tearfully. The Countess had always been a woman of strength and Lady Christine had looked up to her as a significant role model in her life but now Cat was becoming concerned.

"Whatever do you mean, Aunt Vera?"

"I don't know what to think, Cat. I think someone is trying to kill me."

"What makes you think that and who would want to harm you?" Cat solicited gently as she reached for the tea pot. The dowager's shaky hand came up from under her blanket holding a flask.

Pouring a finger of Dow's 40 year old Tawny Porto in each of their tea cups. "I...I don't know, dear but I've been feeling poorly of late and the doctor doesn't seem to know what it is. I know, I know. I'm getting old and I have my aches and pains but this is something different. I feel that someone is watching me all the time, I can't seem to get warm yet nurse tells me the room is very warm and I have to keep the curtains closed because the slightest light bothers me. I first noticed it about a month ago and it's getting worse.

Then there's the odd occurrences and sounds. I awakened one morning yester week to find the portrait of my great, great, great grandmother had been disturbed during the night."

"Perhaps the portrait was moved by your staff to clean?" suggested Cat.

"Perhaps, but I am certain it was fine when I went to bed. Then, night before last I was wakened from a sound sleep in the wee hours by something or someone moving about in my sitting room. I thought I saw a ghastly shadow figure with glowing red eyes staring at me from the far corner of the room. I couldn't sleep a wink after that. The next morning my secretary found that my papers had been disturbed on my writing desk. Nothing had been taken."

Christine listened intently as she savoured the fine amber port with warm aromas of nuts, raisins and vanilla and on the palate, flavours of dried fruits and walnuts lead to a long complex finish.

"I'm sure these incidents were nothing more than oversights." Christine was not as sure as her words purported. She hoped she could give her aunt a modicum of peace while she investigated the nocturnal goings-on.

"I'm so glad you're here, Cat. I feel so much better already just knowing you're here."

A knock at the door interrupted the conversation. "Your dinner[24] M' Lady." said the Lady's Maid, Tina Crumpet, as she set a tray of beef and barley soup, toast, a strawberry scone, a pot of honey and tea on the coffee table in front of the Countess.

"Thank you Crumpet. That will be all." said the Countess dismissing the Maid.

After the Maid had gone Cat suggested that she would like to sample her victuals before her Aunt began her meal. "Do you suspect there might be something in the food, Cat? Surely not. Cook has been with me for thirty years."

"How long has your Lady's Maid been employed?" Christine queried.

"She is Cook's daughter and grew up in this house."

Cat leaned over and put her keen sense of smell to work. Next she tasted

---

[24] means lunch in northern England and Scotland

the soup trusting her sensitive palate to detect any toxin present but she could not identify anything untoward so she collected small specimens from each of the items on the tray. Next she went to the Countess' bedside and took one pill from each vile for testing in the lab.

"Don't worry Aunt Vera I'm sure I'll find nothing. This is just precautionary. Enjoy your dinner."

Cat next walked slowly about the rooms stopping at the portrait of the Viscount as a boy. It was reminiscent of The Blue Boy by Thomas Gainsborough except for the period costume. The boy in this portrait wore blue "T" shirt and shorts. Removing the painting from the wall she carefully examined the work of art, the frame and the back of the painting for any anomalies. Then she examined the wall itself but could find nothing. Her highly sensitive eyesight caught minute flecks of paint scattered on the top of the Louis XVI walnut console table beneath the portrait. When she examined them closely she determined they were from the portrait. She gathered these fragments up and placed them in an evidence bag.

Returning the painting to the wall she turned to her aunt saying, "In the meantime make a note of anything unusual and I'll be back to look in on you before bedtime."

"Oh, would you dear? That would be so nice." replied the Countess gratefully.

10 CHIP TOFF

Rain trickled slowly down the window panes like the tears of the families of so many murder victims. Outside the village seemed imbued with an atmosphere of gloom on this overcast morning.

It had been a restless and sleepless night for Detective Chief Inspector Logan Wisdom. His bed was lumpy and seemed to wrap itself around him making him unbearably hot. He always found it difficult to sleep the first night in a strange bed and, of course, it was near impossible to stop his mind from mulling over the case. The face of the murdered man haunted his dreams. It was six a.m. and he was wide awake. He could hear glasses clinking, dishes rattling and water running. The sounds of the Publicans getting ready for a new day.

Swinging his feet over the side of the bed he gathered his toiletries, donned his dressing gown and made his way to the lavatory at the end of the hall. After completing his morning ablutions he dressed and checked his phone for messages. There were two missed calls.

One message was from Sergeant B. Goodman, "Sergeant B. Goodman here, Guv. Just an update on the missing woman, a Ms. Chrystal D. Canter, was found safe and sound."

The second message was from Lady Christine or Cat. Would he ever get passed her station, he wondered? "Hiya. I'm in town and need to see you. I hope you don't mind." this lightened his mood and of course he didn't mind. He would phone her later.

Locking the oak door of his room behind him he proceeded down the hall with its creaking wooden floor. Reaching the top of the staircase he was greeted by the delicious smells of bacon, sausages, toast and coffee. Following his nose he made his way through the reception area and as he entered the dining room he caught sight of an eye-catching vision sitting alone at a table near the window. Cat looked up and was visibly pleased to see the look of pleasant surprise on his face. "I'm delighted to see you, Cat."

Cat welcomed Logan warmly with an affectionate kiss and Logan responded lovingly.

"You might not be so glad to see me when I ask a favour of you."

"Why? What is it Cat?" Logan entreated.

"I arrived yesterday and over tea with my Aunt Vera she recounted how she had been experiencing some, although minor in nature, unexplained and somewhat disconcerting incidents. I promised I would look into them to put her mind at ease."

"What sort of incidents?"

Christine recounted the basis for the Countess' distress and described how she had examined the contents of her aunt's meal and her rooms. Reaching in her pocket Cat withdrew the specimens she had collected for analysis. "I know it is an imposition and I may be asking you to put yourself in an awkward position but, please, could you have these analysed? It would put my aunt's mind at rest and that would mean a lot to me." she pleaded.

Logan became very serious and was quiet for what seemed to Cat an eternity as he pondered what she had just told him and what she was asking of him. Finally, just when Cat thought she could stand it no longer Logan spoke, "I'm glad you brought this to me, Lady Chris... uh, oh, sorry Cat. This may turn out to be nothing more than imagination..."

"I assure you Logan, the Countess, my aunt, is not a woman given to flights of fancy." Lady Christine said sternly.

They were interrupted by the Publican offering the couple breakfast, "Good morning. My name's Bart Ender and I'm yer Publican. What can I get fur ye? The full English? We have a lovely kipper or poached finnan haddie?"

Christine ordered toast and coffee and Logan ordered a bacon and egg butty and coffee take away.

"Now, Cat. You didn't let me finish. This may finish up as mere memory lapse or trick of the mind, however, there may be a connection with my investigation and I would be remiss if I didn't follow up every possible lead." he explained quickly yet with solemnity.

"Oh, I'm sorry. I should have given you a chance.

Do you really think there might be a connection?" a contrite Christine said asking for forgiveness and trying to wheedle information out of him.

"You know I can't share any information about the case I'm working on, Cat."

"But it might help me to know what I should be on the lookout for." she pleaded.

"Sorry, Cat. It's early days. I can't give you anything right now but as soon as I know something. We did get some good news though. I had a call from Sergeant B. Goodman this morning advising me that the missing woman, Ms. Chrystal D. Canter, has been located. She was found wandering along the road through Monks Wood by a man passing through the wood about half five this morning. She was somewhat hypothermic, sore, dehydrated and tired so they've admitted her to Penrith Hospital for observation.

Why don't I take you out to dinner, tonight and we can share our information?"

"Your toast and coffee Madame and for you sir your egg and bacon butty and coffee take away. Will there be anything else?"

"Yes, that's Lady Christine not Madame, Mr. Ender." Christine said curtly, impatient because she had wanted more answers and she didn't like to wait.

"Y...yes M' Lady. I'm sorry M' Lady."

Logan paid the bill saying to Christine, "I'll see you tonight, then?"

"What? Oh, yes. I look forward to it." she replied deep in thought.

Logan stepped out into the cold, drenching rain and climbed into his pride and joy, his Vogue. His thoughts turned to the case. He had several suspects and plenty of woolly clues but he needed a motive, something that would point to the murderer. Lost in thought as he drove through the gloom, the rhythmic winking of the cat's eyes producing an almost hypnotic state, and before he knew it he had crossed the threshold of the dark, foreboding Monks Wood. The gleam of his headlamps caught a flash of motion so fleeting it could have simply been an illusion. He slowed the Vogue and peering through the rain and into the inky darkness of the forest he glimpsed them, like shadows, a man and a massive wolf at his side loping through the trees and then they were gone, vanished like figments of a dream. Had he actually seen what he thought he saw?

Then his blood ran cold as he heard the lingering and spine-chilling howl. Although he would never admit it he accelerated, sprinting to be clear of the wood as quickly as possible. Rounding the final bend he could make out the lights of Monks Hall burning warmly through the thunderstorm, his refuge.

Rushing from the car to the main door of Monks Hall he was met with a towel by Sergeant Goodman. "Watcha, Guv."

"Ta. Good morning Sergeant. Beastly weather." Logan dried his hair and face while the Sergeant rabbitted on about his offspring and the weather. Logan's mind was elsewhere as they walked to the study. Upon reaching the study D.C.I. Wisdom interrupted the Sergeant's blather asking to be brought up to speed. "Now then Sergeant, what have you got for me?"

"Well, Guv, Mr. Ulysses Upman's phone records have been checked, and it turns out he received two calls. One from Miss Amanda Livering Cole at 13:09 that lasted 3 minutes 37 seconds and a second call at 13:16 from Ms. Imelda Czechs that lasted 2 minutes 11 seconds."

"That accounts for his time from 13:00 to approximately 13:18 leaving him ample time to murder the Earl and make good his escape.

What about Benjamin Wolf's lunch in Rolling Downs?"

"Nowt yet, Guv. We're awaiting confirmation from the local bobby, Guv. I called the local phone company to find what calls were made on the Earl's phone around the time he was reported to have made the call to police headquarters and I confirmed with the police dispatcher. The local phone company verified that someone did, indeed, make two calls from the Monks Hall phones. The first was an overseas call at 13:07 to the M. T. Bank, Isle of Man, lasting 4 minutes and 11 seconds. I've got a call into the bank to get the details. The second call was to an untraceable burner phone at 13:12 lasting 1 minute 32 seconds. The tech department was able to establish that the burner phone pinged a local cell tower, meaning it was in this area."

"Interesting. So, we have established Sebastian Monk was still alive at 13:14. Good work, Sergeant. Keep on it.

You said the first call was to a bank on the Isle of Man. Isn't the Manx coat of arms three running legs? That's the mysterious mark on the key I found in the Earl's pocket."

"Right you are, Guv. "

"Oh, and Sergeant."

"Yes, Guv."

"Call Dr. Cutter Guttmann, Pathologist and head of forensics and ask her if they've found DNA on the garrotte other than that of the victim. It may be nothing but I also have a few additional specimens of evidence collected in the Countess Vera Lee Isay Monk's apartment that I need forensics to examine. Tell them it is a matter of some urgency, Sergeant."

"Yes, Guv. Straightaway."

A few minutes later the Sergeant poked his head in the study door to say Dr. Guttmann had completed the autopsy on the body of Sebastian Monk, Earl of Uppington Downs. "It's time we paid Dr. Guttmann a wee visit."

"Right you are, Guv."

Ten minutes later they were standing in the autopsy room listening to the autopsy report. Dr. Guttmann, a smouldering ash blond with soft grey eyes passed the written report to DCI Wisdom. "I've been wondering if I had lost my appeal. Have you been avoiding me, Logan?" she said coyly.

"You are still the most appealing Pathologist I know Cutter. Now about Sebastian Monk?"

"Take a look at this Logan." Dr. Guttmann motioned them towards the body on her table folding back the sheet so that they could observe the wound.

Logan emitted a low whistle. "So he was stabbed as well as garrotted?"

"The stab wound would have been painful but not fatal. It was inflicted sometime Saturday afternoon I'd estimate. The day before he was murdered. Someone wanted him dead."

"Any other little surprises up your sleeve Cutter?"

Dr. Guttmann continued, "The Earl was garrotted as indicated by the ligature marks lower on the neck. It appears to have been the work of someone skilled in the use of that particular weapon as evidenced by the use of a double loop making it exceedingly difficult for the victim to get their fingers behind both cords to stop strangulation and the two sets of knots expertly arranged so that they would significantly occlude both the carotid arteries and jugular veins causing global cerebral ischemia causing cerebral hypoxia. However, the 0.051mm in diameter garrotte made of graphene of incredible tensile strength was tightened with such force it severed his carotid artery, hence the loss of blood, and even incised the trachea.

Unconsciousness would come in approximately seven to fourteen seconds and death would have come within minutes. However it was not the cause of death."

"Thank... What are you saying Doctor?"

"I'm not finished."

"Oh, beg pardon, Doctor."

"His last meal was tea, kippers, scrambled eggs, crumpet and thick cut marmalade, but I found something else. There was a massive dose of tropane alkaloids in his system. He would have been incapacitated within two or three minutes of ingestion and he most certainly would have been dead within a few hours. He would have experienced delirium, usually involving the inability to distinguish reality from fantasy. He would also have experience anticholinergic syndrome. An anticholinergic agent blocks the neurotransmitter acetylcholine in the central and peripheral nervous systems."

Sergeant Goodman tipped his head this way and that with a puppy dog puzzled expression on his face. "Crumbs. What is that when it's at home, then? In simple copper's language if you please Doctor?" he asked.

"The remains of the herb Datura was found in his stomach contents, probably concealed in the tea. Datura is a genus of nine species of poisonous vespertine flowering plants or plants that bloom or open in the evening and belonging to the Solanaceae family or nightshade plant It blocks the signals to the involuntary muscles such as the vascular system, lungs and the heart among many others.

The cause of death was, in fact, poisoning by tropane alkaloids. He was dead before he was garrotted."

"Crikey," exclaimed the Sergeant, "He was murdered twice. Do you suppose it was two different murderers?"

"That, my good Sergeant, is your job, as they say."

Logan put the good Doctor in the picture as to the context of the collected specimens she was about to examine lending a sense of urgency to their examination and the fact that it might be necessary to visit the Countess' apartment.

"Thank you Cutter. I look forward to your findings concerning the items I've left you with. Please bear in mind that we are trying to save a life this time not determine cause of death.

Oh, did you happen to find any DNA other than the victim's on the garrotte?

"I'm glad you reminded me, Logan. Indeed I did. Interestingly there is a familial link to the deceased."

"There's a what?" exclaimed Logan.

"A familial link. The person wielding the weapon was his daughter."

"Well blow me down! Thank you Cutter. Come along Sergeant we have work to do."

Logan thought perhaps it was time to interview Viscount Charles Monk and to pay the Countess a visit. Stepping from the Coroner's into pelting rain they returned to the Hall.

Jarvis appeared in the study doorway holding a tea tray laden with scones, clotted cream and steaming mugs of tea. "Jarvis, you're timing is impeccable."

"I do try, sir. Will there be anything else, sir?"

"This will do nicely, thank you, Jarvis."

Their cores warmed, thirsts quenched and late afternoon hunger pangs satiated they were ready to get back to the investigation.

The storm had passed, the rain stopped and the sun was beaming down lightening his sombre mood as he departed the front doors of Monks Hall on his way to the Countess' apartment. Wanting to get the lay of the land round about the stately home and time to think he took the long way round. He watched the forest wall for any signs of movement as he strolled and then it occurred to him, he had seen the enigmatic figure before. "Well, I'll be gobsmacked." he said a broad smile spreading across his face as he remembered.

Rounding a corner of the house and stepping from the path to the gravel of the car park he chanced to see a dapper individual entering the garages. He went to the open door and looked in just in time to see a nattily dressed gentleman sliding into a Rubino Red Bentley Flying Spur V8 S. He stepped up to the side of the car surprising the car's occupant who let out a yelp exclaiming, "Blimey! Who the blazes are you and what do you want?"

Logan introduced himself, "Good morning. I'm Detective Chief Inspector Logan Wisdom and who might you be?"

"I am Viscount Charles Monk and you will treat me with the respect my station is due." the Viscount said imperiously.

Pompous toff thought Logan but instead said, "Good just the person I came to see.

Where were you between 1:00 and 4:00 o'clock Sunday afternoon?"

"You will address me either as Viscount or Lord and what business is it of yours what my movements were and by who's authority? May I ask?"

"We are looking into the murder of your father the Lord Sebastian Monk. Do you have any reason you don't want to assist us with our enquiries or perhaps you would rather we carry on this conversation at the station, Viscount?" Logan asserted.

"Well, I never! Steady on! You don't think I had anything to do with murdering my own father?"

"It's a matter of routine, sir, to try to get a picture of everyone's movements."

"I see. Well, I was at the track taking a flutter on the ponies, if you must know."

"Can anyone verify this?"

"I had a natter with Jimmy the jockey. He can tell you I was there."

"What time was this natter and was he with you the whole afternoon?"

"Of course not." the Viscount spat. "Wait, just a minute. I still have the stubs. They'll have the date and time stamp on them."

"I'll need to see them, now, please."

"What! Can't this wait? I'm just on my way out."

"No, this cannot wait. I will need to see them at once."

"Oh alright. Don't bite your arm off. They're here in the Bentley somewhere." After several minutes of searching the Bentley the Viscount was able to produce his stubs which clearly indicated bets had been placed on each of the races from 14:10 to 17:25. "And where might I find this, Jimmy the jockey?"

"Whitehaven Racecourse[25], he's retired from actually racing and hangs out around the stables and paddock. He tends to be a bit blinkered when it comes to the Rozzers[26]." the Viscount said with a look of mock conspiratorial Bon Ami.

"Thank you Viscount. That will be all for now." Detective Chief Inspector Wisdom said dismissively.

Logan left the garages in search of Lady Christine. Locating the main door of the Countess' apartment he rang the bell. He didn't have long to wait before the Lady's Maid, Tina Crumpet, opened the door. Logan introduced himself and asked to see her mistress the Countess Vera Lee Isay Monk. "My name is Detective Chief Inspector Logan Wisdom here to see Countess Vera Lee Isay concerning the death of her son, the Earl of Uppington on the Downs. I will need to speak with you later."

"I see, sir. Please wait here and I will see if the Countess is in." the Lady's Maid directed leaving Logan standing in the entrance hall.

Logan began to slowly wander seemingly aimlessly about the hall looking into each of the various rooms that opened onto the hall. He was just scrutinizing the sun room when Lady Christine appeared by his side. "Hiya. Thank you for coming. C'mon Logan I'll introduce you to my aunt. Say, I don't suppose you've had time to sort the specimens I brought you? I know you're going spare[27]."

Logan opened his mouth to respond but was interrupted by shrieking from the direction of the Countess' chambers. They raced from the entrance hall towards her rooms and were met by the Lady's Maid. "It's the Countess. She's shrieked and acting wild.

Nurse!" yelled Tina Crumpet.

Lady Christine was the first to enter her aunt's bedroom. Countess Vera Lee sat slumped over in her chair by the window. Rushing to her side Cat felt for a pulse. "There's a weedy pulse."

---

[25] closed in 1890
[26] UK slang for police
[27] at wits end

75

Suddenly the Countess began to thrash about, wild eyed and visibly distraught. Cat tried to keep her aunt from hurting herself but could not make any sense of her aunt's gibberish.

The nurse came rushing in and together they placed the Countess in her bed. The nurse checked the Countess' vital signs, "The Countess' skin is flushed and her pupils are dilated. She's running a fever and her heart rate is elevated. She'll go into a coma and cardiac arrest if we don't get her to a hospital fast!"

Within minutes they heard the blare of ambulance sirens as they ground to a halt in the driveway. The paramedics confirmed that the Countess had been poisoned. They stabilized the Countess for transport to the hospital and then they were gone. Leaving Lady Christine feeling helpless and beside herself with rage that there was a villain that would do this to her aunt.

Logan made an effort to console Cat, "Your aunt is in good hands and will be back in her apartment in no time. You need to be with her right now. You go to the hospital while I wait for forensics to arrive.

We need to find the miscreant that perpetrated this heinous act and bring them to justice. I'll brief you on any news as soon as I know something. Now, chivvy along."

"Thank you Logan. I know I can count on you."

Logan looked around for anything that looked out of place or might be the source of poison. He called Sergeant Goodman to come to the Countess' apartment and bring an evidence kit. Then he gathered up the tea things as well as Countess Monk's sherry glass for the Sergeant to submit to Dr. Guttmann for testing.

11 UNDEAD

Floating on a sea of blackness. Not a sound. Not even the beating of her own heart could she hear. Silence in its purest form. Cold dampness surrounded her permeating her to her very core. Unseen things writhed and crawled against her skin and in her hair.

She was asleep she thought. She would wake up soon. So much pain and terror came flooding back. Spectral faces appeared and disappeared. One angry, evil face tormented her soul. "I'm sorry Daddy. I didn't mean to make a mess. I'll clean it up. No! Don't, Daddy!"

A shining, angelic face materialized speaking softly, "It's alright my sweet. It will all be over soon. No more pain. No more fear. No more anger." Then abruptly the light was gone and the angelic face had become ashen and the eyes lifeless. Rage burned within her like a wild fire.

Suddenly she heard it. Like a base drum and the rhythmic pulsing rushing sound in her ears. Her heart had begun to beat once again. It was deafening in the profound silence.

Her lungs were straining for air but pressure from all sides restricted even the most minute movement. The immediate comprehension of her predicament burst into her consciousness like the brilliance of a lightening flash. She was buried alive!

She began to wriggle and squirm in panic. Opening her mouth for air it only filled with dirt choking her. Her scrabbling fingers finally broke the surface. Exploding upward from her shallow grave like a freestyle diver from the depths gasping for sweet resuscitating air.

She retched and sneezed expelling the dirt from her mouth, throat and airway. Relief washed over her and her emerald green eyes filled with tears that began to trickle uncontrollably down her cheeks like tiny rain drops until the fury burning within her reared its ugly head taking back control of her emotions.

No one had seen her pass through the village. Her arrival at Monks Hall at 14:00 hadn't gone completely unnoticed. She thought she had glimpsed a furtive movement in the window of the drawing room and the curtains seemed to move unnaturally and she felt she was being watched.

Sebastian's eyes had betrayed his evil heart as he leered at her. She knew then she was going to kill him. She wanted him to suffer as they had. Now was not the time. She had a mission to complete.

He turned his back to her as he examined her tribute.

Her self control was weakening rapidly. Flashbacks of the horrors he had inflicted on the family. Before she realized it the stiletto, glinting in the sunlight streaming through the sitting room windows, was in her hand. Without thinking she thrust the razor sharp blade unconsciously for his heart but hadn't counted on his agility and strength. Everything seemed to move in slow motion as he sidestepped causing her to miss her intended target and throwing her off balance. The blade pierced his side nicking one of his ribs but, in fact, was no more than a flesh wound. Grabbing her hand he had wrenched the weapon from her grasp as his free hand had connected solidly with her jaw stunning her. He then proceeded to throttle her with his bare hands.

As she sank beneath the waves of unconsciousness her last thought was that of failure.

Dumping her unceremoniously in the boot of her Venitia Sebastian drove her into the village and parked the car down a side street out of sight. He had left her unconscious body in the boot and taken a short cut walking hurriedly back to Monks Hall planning to return later to sort her out properly. He had guests arriving any time now.

After greeting his guests and seeing that everyone was comfortable he made his excuses and left the Hall. He had come back and assuming she was dead he had driven into Monks Wood by back roads. Finding an isolated location he opened the boot and she had tried to escape but she was stiff and groggy from the cramped quarters and limited oxygen of the boot. Exclaiming, "You are a resilient little vixen, aren't you." as he squeezed the life out of her again.

Sinking into oblivion she no longer had any sense of time, space or even of existing. He removed her seemingly lifeless body from the car boot and carried her into the woods. He dug a shallow grave and rolled her in. Backfilling the grave and covering it with leaves and branches to look undisturbed. He left her for dead, buried ignominiously in an unmarked grave in the woods turning his back and walking away as if her life had meant nothing.

Now she felt triumphant. She had cheated death and lived to fight another day. She felt her mission had been given righteous sanction.

Fortunately her attacker had thrown her purse into the grave with her. Dusting herself off and removing the twigs and leaves from her auburn hair Cornett D. Canter backfilled and covered her grave hiding it from any would be rescuers she returned to the Hall through a long forgotten passageway. Soundlessly she had appeared behind Sebastian as he sat in his chair in the library his hand on the phone as if he was about to make a call. Clutching the fine, graphene garrotte she summoned all of her assassin training. So swiftly and skilfully did she place the loops over his head and around his throat he didn't even have time to react before she pulled the lethal snare taught cutting off life giving oxygenated blood flow to his brain. Simultaneously the weapon sliced through his larynx preventing the slightest sound from being uttered.

She knew her car had been impounded and that the police were searching for her. She calculated that the prudent tactic would be to deliver herself into their hands. A good offense is often the best defence. It was early Monday morning before she stepped onto the road winding through Monks Wood. It wasn't long before a car slowed down and stopped beside her its occupant enquiring, "Do you need help, Miss? Can I offer you a lift into the village?"

She was taken to the local constabulary where the gobsmacked Bobby called the paramedics and then called Sergeant B. Goodman.

12 DREAD SPREAD

Duchess Cassandra gazed transfixed at the shafts of sunlight radiating through the west windows of the drawing room as if heralding a celestial arrival. The warmth of the sun in the room was making everyone in the room lethargic. The pervading atmosphere of the room was that of gloom, fear and distrust. Each one acutely aware of the movements of the others.

"Well, I think I need a drink. Would anyone else like one? I'm pouring." offered Benjamin.

"Thanks, old chap, but if it's all the same, I'll pour my own." replied Ulysses.

"What? Don't be daft. You think I'd try to poison you? What possible motive would I have to poison you?

What about you Cassandra?" coaxed Ben.

"Ta. I'll have a Pimm's and lemonade, Ben, and hold the poison." she replied cheekily.

"Very funny. I don't know why you're all pointing fingers at me." Ben rejoined testily.

"No need to get shirty, old man. I think we're all a bit on edge. Say, where's Dr. Boring gotten to?" enquired Ulysses.

"That's odd. He was here a minute ago. Perhaps he's taking another kip somewhere?" suggested Duchess Cassandra.

"Cor blimey! Maybe he's done a bunk. Anyroad, I know I want to get out of this place. I've got better things to do with my time than sit around here like a sitting duck waiting to be picked off by some barmy killer." grumbled Ulysses, his common vernacular exposing where he had come from.

"I'm not sitting around waiting to find out Dr. Dull has been murdered too. I'm going to look for him." declared Ben.

"I'm going with you." proclaimed Duchess Cassandra.

"You're not leaving me here by myself." whinged Ulysses as he rose to join the search party.

Benjamin lead the trio from the drawing room out into the hall going straightaway to the library. The police tape was still across the door and fingerprint dust remained in evidence on the door knobs. "I don't think he went through these doors from the look of the door knobs." Ben reasoned, heading for the study.

Just as the little troupe were about to enter the study a voice behind them made everyone jump, "May we help you?" asked Sergeant Goodman.

"Y... you startled us Sergeant. We were just looking for Dr. Boring. He seems to have wandered off." replied Benjamin.

"I'm sure he's somewhere about. Why don't you all just relax in the drawing room while I have a little shufti."

The Sergeant poked his head through the door of the study and seeing there was no one in there made his way up the staircase to the guests' rooms. Checking each room in turn. Finding the rooms empty he decided to search the grounds. After walking the perimeter of the house and going over the garages he turned to the gardens. Calling the Doctor's name as he strode about the grounds he heard nothing but the fluting, warbling of the robins, the goldfinch's pleasant tinkling medley of trills and twitters, and the incessant buzzing of the bees. Rounding a corner in a rhododendron hedge he came upon the Professor's crumpled form lying at the foot of a garden bench. Rushing over the Sergeant knelt down and quickly removed a length of graphene line from around the Doctor's throat and in so doing he heard a faint, laboured breathe. He immediately felt for a pulse and found it weak and irregular.

Once he had checked for vital signs he supported Boring's neck with his tunic in case of spinal trauma and then checked his airway for obstruction. Then, Sergeant Goodman rapidly dialled 999 urgently requesting an ambulance. Next he called D.C.I. Wisdom to apprise him of the incident.

Logan had been on his way to Penrith Hospital to interview Miss Chrystal D. Canter when he received the call from the Sergeant. He made the full circle on the next roundabout and headed back to Monks Hall. The interview with the heiress would have to wait.

The wait for the emergency team seemed endless but, in reality, was only a matter of minutes before help arrived. The wail of the approaching sirens sent a shock wave of panic through the trio.

"Blimey, what's happened this time? I'm getting well shot from this beastly house of horrors. They've no right to keep us cooped up here just waiting to be murdered in our sleep." hysteria was creeping into Ulysses' voice. His fingers searched his waistcoat pocket in vain for his gold sovereign that he habitually rolled across his fingers for assurance.

"Get a grip on yourself Ulysses. You big girl's blouse. Show a little bottle. Here, get this brandy down you for your nerves." admonished Benjamin as he poured brandy into a glass.

"I'll call Jarvis to bring us some tea.

It is odd though, don't you think? Why would anyone wish harm to a philosopher?" Duchess Cassandra reflected.

They watched as the paramedics arrived and then departed transporting Dr. Boring to waiting emergency physicians, with lights flashing and sirens blaring they were gone in a cloud of dust and gravel flying in all directions.

Once Sergeant B. Goodman had placed the cord in an evidence bag and inspected the area for further evidence he joined the threesome in the drawing room to relate what had occurred and allay any fears. After he had answered their questions he assured them that they would be safe if they stayed together in one spot. They were in the good hands of the police. He also explained that the sooner they caught the nasty piece of work the sooner they could rest easy in the knowledge the villain could no longer hurt anyone and they could go back to their lives.

"So, if there is anything you can tell me, even the smallest detail or what you might think is an insignificant observation please don't keep it to yourself. We don't know what might help us to apprehend the yob." he explained.

They all looked at each other but no one spoke. The Sergeant said, "Right then, I'll leave you to think over what I said. I'll be around and I've called for a support team. They should be here soon." and with that he left the room.

Duchess Cassandra looked at Benjamin, "Ben, if you know something, anything at all please tell the Sergeant. Our lives may be at stake here. Please." she pleaded.

"Me? What makes you so sure I know anything about this. I'm in just as much danger as either of you. Perhaps more. Are you quite sure there isn't something you want to share with the good Sergeant?"

Ulysses sat in subdued silence. "Oh, why don't you two belt up. Our lives are in danger and all you two can do is point fingers and bicker. One of us might be the murderer. Had either of you thought of that?"

"I'm going to call Jarvis to bring us some tea to calm our nerves so we can think rationally." said Duchess Cassandra but before she could ring Jarvis appeared from out of nowhere as if he simply materialized in thin air with a tray containing tea scones, clotted cream and strawberries. The delectable repast seemed to transport the group, temporarily, to a happier place.

Meanwhile, out in the garden, Sergeant Goodman was studying the bench and surrounding area for any further clues while he awaited forensics and a security support team to watch over Duchess Cassandra, Ulysses Upman and Benjamin Wolf.

Logan ground to a halt on the gravel drive in front of the main doors to the huge edifice and bounded from the car. Reaching the Sergeant's side demanding an account of the incident. At that moment the forensics team arrived with the security detail right behind.

"We'll continue this conversation in the study, Sergeant, shall we." directed D.C.I. Wisdom.

"Yes Guv'nor. But, before we go you will want to see these." the Sergeant said, holding out two evidence bags. One containing the garrotte and the other a gold sovereign.

"Hmm, the garrotte has a double knot. One knot on each side of the victim's neck thus closing both the carotid artery and the jugular vein carrying blood to and from the brain at the same time as constricting the airway cutting off oxygen. Slower and more excruciating than breaking the neck. Very nasty indeed." Logan put forward.

"I've seen this coin or one very much like it. Mr. Ulysses Upman has a nervous habit of rolling one across his fingers. We need to see if forensics can find a print on the coin and hopefully two kinds of DNA on the garrotte. See that Dr. Guttmann gets these will you Sergeant." D.C.I. Wisdom directed.

"Dr. I. M. Boring wasn't dead. The killer didn't finish the job, Sergeant. Why do you think that is?"

"I think I might have interrupted the killer, Guv."

"I see. Well, it's too late to make the journey to Penrith to interview Miss Canter. I'll call the hospital to make sure she will still be in and go first thing tomorrow. I need a cuppa and I imagine you could use one yourself, Sergeant. Let's go inside. You speak to Jarvis about the tea and I'll make a call to the Penrith Hospital. Then we'll have another chat with the 'Three Amigos'".

"Yes sir, Guv'nor. Right you are." said the amiable Sergeant.

"Oh, Sergeant?"

"Yes, Guv?"

"Do a background check on Chrystal D. Canter. I want everything you can find."

"Right you are, Guv."

Logan went into the study to call Penrith Hospital to confirm that Miss Chrystal D. Canter would still be there in the morning for his interview. He was gobsmacked when he learned she had checked herself out, against the doctor's better judgement, within four hours of having been admitted at 6:45 that morning.

He called dispatch straight away to issue a BOLO (Be On Look Out) for Chrystal D. Canter.

Sergeant Goodman entered the room carrying a tray holding their cuppa, a plate of raisin scones and clotted cream. "Thank you Sergeant that will hit the spot.

I've just learned that Miss Canter voluntarily released herself from the hospital at about 10:15 and has gone missing. I've issued a BOLO."

"Crumbs" exclaimed the Sergeant. Then he was quiet as he drank his tea. He was so deep in thought he didn't even notice the scone he had just dispatched had been so light and flaky it had simply melted in his mouth and how luscious and fresh the strawberries had been. When he had finished he wondered aloud, "Guv'nor, you don't think she could have come back here do you?"

"That is certainly a possibility, Sergeant.

Well, I think I'll check with the hospital to see if they've determined what caused the Countess' infirmity then I'll speak briefly with our trio.

Confirm that our Protection Detail is in place and on high alert, will you Sergeant."

"Right, Guv."

Logan wasn't on the phone long before he thanked the attending physician and hung up looking worried he left the study in search of the three guests.

Entering the drawing room he addressed the trio, "You are aware that Dr. I. M. Boring has been found in the garden having been the victim of an assault. He is in intensive care in the hospital in guarded condition. If you don't want to help us at least help yourselves. If there is anything you know that you've been keeping to yourself or even the most trivial detail you might have noticed that seemed out of place or in some way unusual now would be a good time to share it."

"How long are you going to keep us here like this? Just waiting. Waiting for what? To be murdered?" Ulysses bleated. The icy fingers of panic starting to take hold again.

"Get a grip old man." said Benjamin. "We're safe here with police protection."

"I'm going back to the study in case anyone would like to talk privately."

Ulysses sat trembling in silence looking like a frightened child. Duchess Cassandra went over to try to comfort the real estate tycoon.

Benjamin, appearing to have come to a decision, got to his feet saying, "I'm going for a walk to clear my head and think." He didn't go far. Knocking on the open study door he stepped into the room to find D. C. I. Wisdom seated comfortably behind an expansive mahogany English partner's desk, with a handsome moulded top inset of gilt embossed red leather.

"Close the door Mr. Wolf. Won't you join me in a whiskey? It's a fine single malt."

"Yes, thank you I think I will."

Logan poured two fingers of the golden nectar into each of two cut lead crystal tumblers and handed one to Ben. The two men sat sipping their drinks sizing each other up. After a moment Logan spoke, "What have you come to tell me Mr. Wolf?"

"I am, by nature, a particularly careful man DCI Wisdom. This has been of great advantage in my chosen vocation. I've been described by some as an Illusionist of sorts. I have acquired a certain skill set that others have found invaluable when they became aware they were in dire straits."

"What do you mean an Illusionist of sorts? And just what might this skill set be, exactly, and what sort of people and circumstances are we talking about, Mr. Wolf?" asked an intrigued DCI Wisdom.

"Let's just say that I have a special gift for making people and things disappear, reappear and even transform them into distinctly dissimilar entities.

I have, on occasion, been pressed into service by our government and others as well as various law enforcement services but above all I endeavour to help individuals and families with nowhere else to turn.

I'm a sucker for lost causes, Detective Chief Inspector." Ben smiled self-consciously.

"Yes, well, be that as it may, it all sounds rather dodgy to me. Anyroad, just how do you think you can assist us in our investigation, Mr. Wolf?"

"It began a couple of months back. I noticed things out of place in my home. Little things. Nothing significant in and of itself. Things only I would notice. Nothing was ever taken. It was as if someone wanted me to know they had been my home, invading my space and could do so at will.

Then there were the unnaturally long glances in my direction at restaurants and on the street and if I took a second look the mystery person would be gone. In fact, just as I left my cottage I noticed a footprint in my garden under my kitchen window as if someone had been peering in.

I felt that someone was following me on my trek to Monks Hall."

"It sounds to me like you're allowing your imagination to runaway with you, Mr. Wolf."

"I assure you, DCI Wisdom, that thought has crossed my mind many times. However, I should tell you that Picov Andropov, Dr. I. M. Boring and, indeed, the Earl Sebastian Monk had all come to me for my help."

"Hmm, I see. That's a horse of a different colour, indeed, Mr. Wolf. What sorts trouble were these people in and what exactly was it that you did for them?" DCI Wisdom said suspiciously.

"That would be a breach of confidentiality and my personal and professional ethics not to mention endangering lives and a contravention of the Official Secrets Act."

"Why are you telling me this now?"

"Because I'm afraid the killer is not finished, DCI Wisdom."

"Do you have any idea where the killer might strike next?"

"Yes, DCI Wisdom, I think I may be the next target."

13 BAT APPEARS

A day had passed since Logan had spoken to Lady Christine and he was getting anxious to learn how her aunt was progressing. He climbed wearily into his Vogue drove to the hospital where the Countess had been admitted. Entering the front doors his senses were assaulted by hospital odours of disinfectant and sickness, a sea of white, the hustle and bustle of nurses, doctors, staff and patients and the sounds of discomfort emanating from various rooms up and down the corridor.

His first port of call when he arrived was to the emergency admitting where he learned that Dr. Boring's wound had been superficial. They were keeping him in overnight for observation but he was due to be released the next morning if all was well.

He had learned in a brief phone conversation with the attending physician that a build up of tropane alkaloids specific to Datura belladonna or Devil's Trumpet had been found in Countess' blood and tissue samples and coupled with her signs of delirium and hallucinations she was dangerously close to slipping into a coma. The physician had gone on to say that she had been very fortunate because they might not have detected the poison until it was too late had it not been for her agitated state.

Logan located Lady Christine beside her aunt's bed. When she saw Logan a radiant smile spread over her face like beaming sunshine and rising from her chair she wrapped her arms around his neck proclaiming, "I'm so very glad to see you, Logan. The doctors say that Aunt Vera Lee will be up and around in a couple of days."

"That's brilliant Cat. I can't tell you how much I needed some good news. But you're not looking convinced. How are you holding up? You look exhausted. Are you hungry?"

"I'm famished."

"Good! Your aunt is resting peacefully. Let me take you to dinner and then home for a good night's sleep. You can come back in the morning refreshed."

"That sounds marvellous. Where are we going? I must look a mess. I can't go out like this can we make a quick stop at Monks Hall so I can change and freshen up?"

"I discovered a quiet little place the Bake & Entrée. Sure we can swing by Monks Hall but, for the record, you look smashing just the way you are."

Cat smiled and blushed self-consciously.

They both needed to unwind and an evening out was just the ticket. It was clear that Logan was smitten and for the next few hours his mind would be on nothing but Cat.

They drove back to Monks Hall in comfortable silence. The light of day drained away until the twilight stole away the vibrant colours of the day. The warm glow of the sun's retreating rays made Cat's hair blacker, her skin softer and her eyes bigger. The trees that lined the lanes cast lengthening shadows like giant sentries. The fading light sent the birds to their roosts for the night and the crickets came out to serenade the contented couple on their travels. Approaching the ancient mansion the remaining blaze from the gradually dimming sky danced along the glass windows.

Lady Christine entered her aunt's apartments and as she ascended the staircase to her room Viscount Charles Monk called from the foyer, "Ah, you've returned at last. How is dear old grandmamma?"

"Do you honestly expect me to believe you care? You would know if you had the common decency to take the time to visit or even call the hospital Aunt Vera Lee is on the mend. She'll be home in a few days." she called over her shoulder as she reached the top of the staircase.

After washing and dressing Lady Christine descended the winding staircase and walking through the entrance hall she thought she glimpsed motion in her aunt's chambers. She reached her aunt's rooms in a flash and there sitting comfortably in the dimly lit room was her brother, Bartholomew (Bat) Tussilago and sitting patiently at his side was Bailey. "Watcha. How have you been and, more interestingly, how is DCI Wisdom?" he teased with a cheeky smirk.

Cat ruffled Bailey's ears and stroked his broad head. "Patience is not about how long you wait it's about how you behave while you wait." thought Bailey to no one in particular.

"What are you doing here? I thought you were off in Europe chasing villains?

I suppose you haven't heard about Aunt Vera Lee?" Christine A. Terry or Cat replied, ignoring her brothers jibe.

"I've just come from her bedside as have you, sister dearest. I'm just having a little shufti.

You'd best be getting back to your dinner engagement before DCI Wisdom gets tired of waiting."

Just then Logan entered the room. "We'll ha... Blimey! Sir James, champion!" he exclaimed reaching down to pat Bailey's shoulder and given him a hug. "Who's a good boy?"

"What if I never find out who's a good boy?" thought Bailey.

"Bat, please Logan." Sir James grimaced.

"Forgive us Bat, but we're at risk of losing our dinner reservations. Will you be in the area long?"

Bat allowed as he would be around. Logan said, "We'll have to chivvy along if we are to get a table." Then Lady Christine and Logan left for their dinner engagement.

The romantic classics of Elgar's Salut d'Amour, Rota's Romeo and Juliet and others played softly in the background as the couple unhurriedly enjoyed their meal and each other's company. After a sumptuous dinner and over glasses of a silky and rich port with a caramel aroma the couple gazed into each other's eyes as their relationship developed into something truly special.

Logan's phone began to vibrate alerting him to an incoming call. "Sorry Cat but I have to take this." The voice on the other end was that of Sergeant Goodman. "Sorry to disturb, Guv'nor."

"Yes, what is it Sergeant? Don't faff about Sergeant."

"Right you are, Guv. I have the results of the lab tests of the Countess' tea things and sherry glass, Guv. Traces of tropane alkaloids were found in the sherry glass but not enough to have been lethal. It was also found in the honey and her flask of port."

"Cheers Sergeant. Did the doctor happen to mention any other method of administering the poison? Email me the report and then get yourself off home to your family and I'll see you bright and early."

"Yes, Guv, she said it could have been administered topically. I'll send you the report right away, Guv. Good night, Guv."

Logan had been looking at Christine while he was in conversation with the Sergeant. She knew something was afoot. "What is it Logan? What have you learned? Is it something to do with Aunt Vera Lee?"

"Yes. Dr. Guttmann has found traces of tropane alkaloids in your Aunt's port."

"But I had a shot of the port

"We've got to get back to your aunt's apartment. There may be other sources of the toxin." Logan quickly settled up their account and they left the restaurant.

When they arrived at Monks Hall they saw a light in one of the Countess' windows. Alighting from the Vogue they hurried into the apartment to find Chip looking sheepish like the proverbial child caught with his hand in the cookie jar. "Hiya Cat. I wasn't expecting you back so soon. The DCI not what you expected?" Chip jeered with a smarmy smirk on his face.

"What are you doing in here?" Cat asked sternly.

"I... I thought I heard something and came in to check. And anyroad I have every right to be in here. She's my Grandmamma, after all." he whined.

"What's that in your hand Viscount?"

"None of your business."

"May I remind you this is a murder enquiry, Viscount. Everything is my business. Now, I'll ask you again. What do you have in your hand?"

"Well, if you must know it's my aunt's moisturizing cream. My skin was feeling a little dry and I thought it might help."

"I'll take that Viscount. This is a possible crime scene and nothing may be removed so I'll need to check your pockets. Please place the contents of your pockets on the table, now." ordered Logan sternly as he stood with his hand out waiting.

"It's just moisturizer." bleated Chip as he reluctantly handed over the moisturizing cream and huffily emptied his pockets of their contents.

Logan had put on latex gloves and placed the jar of cream into and evidence bag. "I see nothing here of interest. You may gather up your belongings. Now, if you would please leave the Countess' rooms I can get to work."

"You have your own suite if you want to entertain your toy boy." Chip chided as he retreated from his aunt's rooms.

"Cat, we need to search these rooms and gather up everything your aunt could have ingested, applied topically, injected or inhaled and get it all to the lab for testing. Then we must ascertain who either provided the item or had access to have tampered with it.

Put these gloves on. We have to be careful how we handle evidence as I'm sure you are aware."

Lady Christine's eyes were drawn to the portrait enshrined in the alcove her eyes coming to an abrupt halt at a ghastly gaping gash across the boy. Her audible gasp caught Logan's attention. Turning he saw what had caused Cat's exclamation.

"Who would have done such a thing?" Cat blurted out. "The only ones in my Aunt's apartments were Chip and the staff."

Logan walked carefully across the alcove making certain not to disturb anything. Examining the alcove as he walked with a high powered torch. Nothing else seemed out of place. Reaching for his phone he dialled the Scene of Crime squad and told them their services were required. "Cat you should get some rest you look exhausted. I'll stay here until forensics have finished with the scene. Do you have any idea at all who might have wanted to do this, Cat?"

"No, Logan. There is no one I can think of but perhaps Chip is the one you should be talking to."

"Hmm. I'll speak with him first thing tomorrow."

Sometime later SOCO arrived going over the scene with a fine tooth comb. The evidence recovery team member removed the painting after photographing it in situ. She printed the portrait and frame, then as she did so she noticed the corner of a piece of paper peeking out from the gash. Removing it she placed it in an evidence bag. DCI Wisdom noticed this and asked, "What have you there?"

"Papers secreted between the canvas and paper backing." replied the officer as she handed the evidence bag to DCI Wisdom.

"You've dusted it for finger dabs, have you?"

"Yes sir."

"Good." Logan said as he carefully accepted the evidence pouch containing the papers for later examination. "I will need to keep these for now. I'd like your report as soon as possible."

"Yes sir." responded the team leader.

14 SECRETS

After breakfast the next morning Logan walked briskly down the Toadspool in the Dell high street to the local constabulary headquarters. The breeze was soft and cool and filled with the honey scent of the buddleia and citrus fragrance of the magnolia.

He entered the white washed stucco walls with navy blue trim of the station house where just inside the burly and affable Sergeant B. Goodman greeted him with a hearty, "All right, Guv'nor."

DCI Wisdom responded, "I'm super good Sergeant but I'll get better. What have you been able to learn about Chrystal D. Canter?"

"The file is waiting for you in interview room one, Guv."

Logan sat at a table in interview room number 1. The room smelled of stale cigarette smoke, the floors were randomly patterned by mystery stains and cigarette burns and the paint on the grimy walls had begun to peel. He never liked to commandeer someone else's space. It never set well with the individual displaced no matter how easy going they were and even though they might not object. Anyroad he didn't like always having to ask where this or that was.

On the table in front of him lay the forensics report on samples taken from the Countess' apartments and the background report on Chrystal D. Canter.

Opening the forensics report he found what he had suspected. They had found a low concentration of aconite in each of the cosmetic containers and the sherry. The report stated that each item taken individually would cause illness but not death however, taken cumulatively death would be a certainty. The scientists had discovered the source of the alkaloid to be that of the poisonous plant, monkshood.

Monkshood is also known as wolfsbane, friar's cap and granny jump out of bed among others. Its botanical name is aconitum napellus. All parts of the plant especially the roots contains the alkaloid, aconitine, a deadly poison that paralyzes.

The report went on to state that the only finger prints recovered from the items were those of the Countess and Viscount.

Was it the Viscount? He was too obvious. He couldn't believe what he was thinking. More often than not the obvious answer was the right answer. Who else had a motive for eliminating the Countess?

He turned next to the report on Chrystal D. Cantor and was gobsmacked to see the label across the folder in bold block letters "CONFIDENTIAL SEALED". He flipped open the folder to find the reports of relentless domestic abuse, murder and a missing person. There were physical descriptions and photographs of the twins Chrystal and Cornett, their mother Brandy and her spouses Alvaro and Sebastian.

The murder had been that of Brandy's second husband, Alvaro Canter. Though he was found face down in a vat of wine there was no wine found in his lungs. The forensics report showed distinct indications of aconite poisoning. The pathologist went on to state that Alvaro had been garrotted.

The report of the investigating team had Brandy on the list of suspects. Other suspects included the twins: Chrystal and Cornett, and Alvaro's brother, Pablo. However, the investigators were most interested in the Earl of Uppington on the Downs, Sebastian Monk although nothing was ever proven.

Pablo and Sebastian appeared to have iron clad alibis. Although the alibis were checked neither alibi was ever fully tested.

Brandy D. Canter had gone missing and perhaps was on the run after murdering her husband.

The twins were twenty four years of age by this time and did not have solid alibis. However, after questioning the twins, detectives determined that it would be prudent to bring in a psychologist for an opinion of the twins psychological condition. The twins had consented to psychological profiles by Dr. E. Ville.

A Confidential Psychological Report was included in the file folder.

The report had been compiled by Chartered Clinical Psychologist, Dr E. Ville, specialist in psychological trauma. Dr. E. Ville stated, for the record, that he had been jointly instructed by El Cuerpo Nacional de Policia, Spain's National Police and the twins legal guardian, Alvaro Canter to assess whether the twins suffered a formal psychological or psychiatric disorder as a result of the series of traumatic events.

One of the most prevalent consequences of childhood abuse is post traumatic stress disorder (PTSD).

It was the considered opinion of Dr. E. Ville that the twins had processed the trauma experienced in uniquely different ways. Chrystal exhibited no obvious dysfunctional disorders of the trauma suffered. She experienced nightmares, depression and anxiety in the past but appeared to be symptom free currently.

Cornett, however, exhibited a more severe clinical profile, emotional avoidance considered an unhealthy coping strategy. There had been periods of substance abuse and psychosis, suicide attempts and hallucinations. The prognosis was that there had been little improvement to date despite being referred for counselling. She requires cognitive behavioural therapy.

Brandy was never found and the case remains unsolved and open. There was a side note that Alvaro's brother Pablo had even employed a missing persons investigator from Tel Aviv, Yahuda Guy, said to be the best in the business, to locate Brandy D. Canter. The crack investigator traced a woman to an institution for the insane that witnesses swore bore a striking resemblance to Brandy D. Canter but was unable to bring to light any further leads.

There was a knock at the door, "Yes?" called DCI Wisdom.

Sergeant Goodman entered the interview room. "I've just received word from the Isle of Man that the small key is not one of theirs, Guv."

"What do you know about the triskelion, Sergeant?"

"Nowt, sir. It's the Isle of Man symbol. More than that I can't say."

"The triskelion or triad is an ancient symbol consisting of three legs or lines radiating from the centre. The triad attributes are thought to represent: creation, preservation and destruction or motion, evolution and illumination. The triad is also embodied in the Roc sign produced when you hold out your palms while touching your thumbs and index fingers forming a triangle. It's an important illuminati symbol signifying the few ruling the many power structure. When the triad is placed over an all seeing eye it becomes more powerful."

"What's this illuminati when it's at home then, Guv?" asked the Sergeant, intrigued.

DCI Wisdom explained, "Well, Sergeant, you may find this hard to accept, but it is an organization of world leaders, business authorities, innovators, artists and other influential members of the global community. They are alleged to conspire to control world affairs by masterminding events and planting agents in positions of the greatest power with the goal of establishing a New World Order. This insidious organization has its stealthy tentacles hidden from view in everything we do."

"Cor blimey. You don't think we're looking at a sinister conspiracy do you, Guv?" the Sergeant asked with a worried look on his face.

"What I think Sergeant is that we need to go over the study, library and the Countess' chamber again but this time with a fine tooth comb. Do you think you could locate the architectural drawings of this pile?"

"I'll do my best, Guv'nor."

With that Logan left the police station and made his way back to Monks Hall. He was met at the entrance by the deceased Earl of Uppington Downs butler, Jarvis. "Good morning Detective Chief Inspector. May I offer you tea, sir?"

"Good morning Jarvis. Tea would be brilliant, thank you. I'll be in the study."

"Very good sir."

Logan had just entered the study when Jarvis appeared at the side of the desk with a tea tray bearing tea and flaky, melt in your mouth raison scones and clotted cream. "Shall I pour, sir?" Logan nodded his consent. Jarvis tipped a little cream in the tea cup, poured the tea and added two teaspoons full of sugar stirred and then asked, "Will that be all, sir?"

"Ta, Jarvis. You are a marvel. Please see that I'm not disturbed."

"As you wish, sir."

Logan sipped his tea while he meticulously scanned every inch of the room. He observed a photograph of the Earl dressed in full formal Scottish highland regalia standing beside the president of the United States and each appeared to be forming the Roc symbol. Not perceiving any anomalies he began to walk slowly around the perimeter pushing here and there on the walls and trim. Then pulling books from the bookshelves without the slightest result.

He went next door to the library and again stood painstakingly scrutinizing every inch of the library walls, ceiling and floor for anomalies without success. Logan was alerted to a faint scraping sound. Unexpectedly a massive oak bookshelf in the wall behind the chair Sebastian had been seated in when he was murdered began to move ever so slightly. Logan watched in wrapt fascination as the wall opened up to reveal Sir Bartholomew Tussilago. "All right, Logan?"

"Watcha, Bat. So that's how it was done."

"This old house is a rat's warren of passages and tunnels." remarked Bat.

A doggie sneeze was heard from the darkness, then Bailey, shaking his head to clear it, appeared behind Bat. "This house is protected by killer dust bunnies." Bailey thought to no one in particular.

"Who would know about the passage? Surely Sebastian would have heard the movement of the door?" thought Logan out loud.

"Not if the murderer lay in wait, secreted somewhere in the room before Sebastian entered. Then exited the room by the secret passage." suggested Bat.

Bat watched as Logan scrupulously re-examined the panel for triggers. He was down on his knees running his fingers along the baseboard and was just about to give up frustrated his fingers detected the slightest irregularity. Pressing a tiny section of trim he heard a barely detectible click of a latch.

"It would be helpful to obtain an architectural plan of the secret passages that honey comb this building." said Logan but when he looked up Sir Bartholomew had vanished.

Closing the panel he went in search of Sergeant Goodman. He found the good Sergeant in the study seated in front of his computer with a self-satisfied smile on his face. "Well, Sergeant, what seems to have you smiling like the proverbial Cheshire Cat?"

"Oh, hello Guv'nor. I searched the internet and found the architects of the Monks Hall to be Adrian Roman and Domus Villa partners in the firm of A. Roman Villa Architects and Interior Design LLP. I gave them a bell and they emailed me the drawings."

"Well done, Sergeant. Transfer them to your tablet so we can take them with us as we explore the secret passages."

"Right you are, Guv. Oi, did you say secret passages?" the burley Sergeant asked apprehensively.

"I did indeed, Sergeant." The pair left the study going through into the library. Sergeant Goodman watch as DCI Wisdom, standing very close to the wall behind the chair they had found the Earl's lifeless body in and carefully placed the toe of his shoe on the baseboard. The good Sergeant stood gobsmacked as he watched the book case begin to move.

They donned headlamps and Logan armed with a brilliant hand torch prepared to enter the passage through the panel in the library. Sergeant Goodman took one look at the dark, narrow passage and whinged, "B...but Guv, it's so small."

He watched as DCI Wisdom slipped into the darkness. The easy-going giant stepped cautiously into the darkness with DCI Wisdom leading the way. Their headlamps lit up panelled walls, wooden floors, and dust. They looked on as the walls and floors appeared to come alive. Cockroaches and centipedes darted and scuttled into cracks and crevices. It was a tight squeeze for the Sergeant's six foot seven inch, twenty and a half stone bulk.

A very nervous Sergeant Goodman didn't notice DCI Wisdom duck and walked straight into a massive spider web causing him to hurriedly retreat, thrashing and flailing his arms trying to rid himself of the clinging, ghostly muddle. Meanwhile, DCI Wisdom had disappeared from view increasing the Sergeant's angst. "Guv'nor? Uh... umm... Guv'nor?"

Barely audible scurrying and scratching sounds could be heard all around conjuring up ghostly visions in the Sergeant's imagination.

"I'm down here Sergeant."

"Down where, sir? I... I can't see your light, sir."

"Follow my voice, Sergeant."

Unexpectedly the Sergeant's headlamp switched off, "Crumbs! My blooming light's on the blink sir!" exclaimed Sergeant Goodman his voice indicating his rising panic.

"Take a deep breath Sergeant and stay where you are. I'm coming to you." Silence seemed to close in around the Sergeant as he stood motionless in the pitch black, waiting, dust filling his nostrils causing him to sneeze. Just as he recovered he felt something land and clamp onto his shoulder putting his pluck to the test and startling the big man to jump higher than one would have thought possible bellowing, "Blimey!" before he could stop it.

"Steady on Sergeant. What's all the palaver, then? Let's have a look at that dodgy headlamp gubbins of yours. Ah, I see the problem. You must have switched it off when you were trying to rid yourself of the cobweb."

"Ta, Guv. What are we looking for, Guv?"

"We need to determine if this passage could have been used by the killer and whether or not any evidence remains.

Let's bash on shall we, Sergeant. We've wasted enough time faffing about." Logan chided as he struggled to turn around in the cramped passageway. They moved forward slowly as they descended. The passage began to get narrower and the ceiling lower until finally just as Logan stepped out of the confining corridor and into a subterranean chamber he heard the whinging rumble of his Sergeant, "Crumbs! Sorry Guv, but I seem to be bunged into this doorway like a stopper in a bottle." There was a groan and a splintering sound as if the ancient structure were coming apart at the seams and just like a cork from a bottle of champagne the Sergeant shot forth into the chamber.

The chamber was a sort of hub with a number of passageways leading off from it. Over one of the openings was a pyramid containing an all seeing eye. Following the drawings on the Sergeant's tablet they were able to find their way to the exterior access point without further incident. When they emerged they found themselves in Monks garden folly.

"I'm not one to complain mind, but if I never have to go back in that black hole of Calcutta with all those creepy crawlies it will be too soon."

The folly was a sandstone pyramid the interior of which was adorned with ornate mouldings depicting pyramids with the all seeing eye and triskelions. There was an inscription carved into the lintel above a doorway leading to an antechamber, "et aquam in sanguinem". Stepping through the doorway DCI Wisdom found a small, windowless room, empty save for a small crystal water feature situated in the centre of the room. The flowing water made a tranquil sound as it murmured and burbled through the pebbles.

"Hmm... How's your Latin Sergeant?"

"Sorry Guv, the only Latin I know is pig Latin. What now, Guv'nor?" enquired the Sergeant.

"Well, Sergeant we've learned how the murder was committed in a locked room. Now we must discover the who and the why and whether or not the murders are in any way connected with the attempt on the life of Countess Vera Lee Isay Monk.

Call SOCO and have them go over the hidden passage and the folly for any forensic evidence.

Let's go find a cuppa to wash this dust away."

"Right you are, Guv."

Logan spotted movement out of the corner of his eye and quickly flicked an enormous centipede that was about to begin its ascent up the Sergeant's neck from his shoulder and stamped on it, startling the big man. "Crumbs!" exclaimed Sergeant Goodman with a shudder.

Thanking his Guv'nor for saving his life the pair returned to the Hall.

15 NOW YOU SEE HER

Returning to the study Logan and the Sergeant were gobsmacked to find Chrystal D. Canter awaiting them. She had auburn hair and dark green eyes, so dark they were like looking into the infinite depths of the sea. She possessed a cold, cruel beauty. Her lips curling into a sardonic smile she said, "I understand you were looking for me?"

"You have lead us a merry chase, Miss Chrystal D. Canter, I must say."

"Yes, well, I'm sorry but it was necessary, I assure you, and my name's not Chrystal D. Canter. That's my twin sister. My name is Cornett D. Canter."

Logan tried not to register surprise but his face betrayed him, "I see. Well, Miss Canter, where have you been all this time?" While he watched her he thought there was something familiar about her but he couldn't put his finger on it.

"I've been a trifle preoccupied running for my life, DCI Wisdom." she claimed cool as a cucumber. Perhaps a little too cool, thought Logan.

Logan sensed that there was something emotionally unusual about the woman. "What makes you think your life is in danger, Ms. Canter?"

"Forgive me but being stuffed in my car boot for hours and then buried alive has that affect on me."

"I think you had better start with why you have turned yourself in to us and why you were here in the first place, Miss Canter."

"Turned myself in? Why, what do you mean, turned myself in? I've done nothing wrong."

"If you've done nothing wrong then why have you been running from us, Miss Canter?" Logan asked incredulously.

"I already told you. I didn't know who I could trust and I was in fear for my life."

"And what has changed now, Miss Canter?" he demanded suspiciously.

"I've had time to think things over and I decided that if I can't trust the police who can I trust."

"You may rest assured I will pursue this issue further. Now if you would explain your presence here at all?"

"I had been summoned by Sebastian Monk."

"Why were you summoned, as you put it? What authority did he have over you?"

"He was blackmailing me. We were to meet at 14:00 Saturday afternoon so that he could extract his tribute."

"What was this, tribute, as you call it? What was it he held over you, Ms. Canter?"

"The bung this time was to be fifty thousand ponds. I'm sorry DCI Wisdom but I'm not going to reveal that information."

"Where did you go after you left your home?"

"I arrived at Monk's Hall at 14:00. I made my tribute and that is when he attacked me. He choked me into unconsciousness and threw me in the trunk of my own car, a black Venitia Z 200 Roadster. He left me in there until he could come back and finish his murderous deed.

When I regained consciousness I had no idea how long I had been out for the count and in the blackness of the boot I had no concept of time. All I know is that when he finally returned and opened the boot I attempted to escape. Unfortunately, laying in a cramped position for so long I wasn't able to put up much of a fight. The brute easily overpowered me and this time he was bent on finishing me off good and proper.

Everything went black and I don't remember anything after that until I found myself buried alive thankfully in a shallow grave. I was able to break free and made my way to the road where a passerby kindly took me to the local constabulary."

"Where have you been since you left the hospital?"

"I... I don't know. I've just been walking and driving around trying to clear my head." Cornett whinged.

Logan noticed he couldn't maintain eye contact with the woman. He observed she often looked up to the right indicating that her responses were fabricated. "I think you are not telling me the truth. I think you went back to Monks Hall and murdered Sebastian Monk."

"Don't be ridiculous. You must think me potty, DCI Wisdom. The fiend had almost killed me twice. Why would I give him another chance? Anyroad, how would I have gotten in without anyone noticing?" she objected.

"You lived here as a small child and probably knew every inch of this place, especially the best hiding places. You used an old forgotten passage into the house and made your way to the library and while you contemplated your next move providence delivered your victim into your eagerly waiting hands.

All you had to do was slip quietly from your place of concealment and creeping up behind the unsuspecting Earl you slipped the garrotte neatly around his throat and pulled it tight." Logan studied her face for any signs of emotion that might reveal her guilt. Her cold, shark-like eyes remained emotionless.

"A very imaginative story DCI Wisdom but if you had a shred of evidence you would have arrested me by now."

"We have SOCO scouring every inch of the folly and the passages for even the slightest of forensic evidence as we speak. Oh, and did I mention? DNA was found on the garrotte with a familial link to his daughter. I'll wager it's yours. What do you think?"

"I think I want my lawyer." replied Cornett.

"Sergeant we will need a DNA kit."

"Right you are Guv'nor." rumbled the Sergeant rising and rummaging in the mobile evidence case.

Sergeant Goodman opened the package removing a cotton tipped swab. "Open up, if you please, Miss." The Sergeant swabbed the inside of Cornett's cheek and placed the cotton swab in its sterile protective vile to be delivered to forensics for testing.

"Sergeant, have two of the uniforms escort Miss Canter to the station to detain her for further questioning."

"Right you are, Guv'nor." he acknowledged reaching for the radio and speaking to one of the uniformed constables. The Woman Police Constable, WPC, entered the study within moments. Putting handcuffs on Cornett she ushered her out of Monks Hall to a waiting police cruiser.

Not long after the constables left with Cornett D. Canter Sergeant Goodman received a frantic radio call. "What do you mean gone, Constable? What are you on about?" bellowed the Sergeant.

"Well Serge, we were enroute to the station and passing through Monks Wood when Alice... ur... I mean Constable A. Kidd turned to check on our prisoner. That's when she noticed."

"Noticed what Constable J. Walker?" demanded the Sergeant, emphasizing "what" trying not to lose his patience.

"Well, Guv, she scarpered. The prisoner just up and vanished, like." whinged the flustered Constable.

"You mean to tell me she escaped a moving vehicle, wearing manacles and being under the very noses of not one but two highly trained Constables?" enquired an incredulous Sergeant, his blood pressure rising by the second.

"Well, Serge, we were doing about forty five miles per hour at the time and the cuffs are laying on the back seat of the cruiser."

"I want full written reports from you both on my desk before you leave. Send up two constables to replace you at Monks Hall and put out a BOLO immediately. You two have made a right dogs breakfast of a doddle." roared Sergeant Goodman.

"Y...yes, Guv. Right you are, Guv. We're sorry, Guv." The radio went quiet.

Sergeant Goodman addressed DCI Wisdom, "Cor blimey. It's all gone pear shaped Guv'nor. She's scarpered."

"Put a search team together Sergeant and search the area starting with Monks Wood and the secret passageways in and around Monks Hall."

"Yes, Sir." said the Sergeant over his shoulder as he left the study to begin the search.

16 BLOOD AND ICE

Tiny dust particles darted and danced in the currents and eddies of the stale air of the room as they floated in the golden rays of the afternoon sun streaming through the sitting room windows. The room was warm and cosy making its occupants lethargic. The only sound was the mind-numbing tick tock of the 1825 Scottish mahogany grandfather clock with a broken swans neck pediment bonnet as motionless as an impassive sentry standing watch over the gloomy little group.

No one spoke. In fact, no one had said a word for what seemed hours. The atmosphere was claustrophobic. The fear and distrust was palpable.

Ulysses was well on his way to being in the bag in an attempt to blunt the rising knife edge of fear. Dr. Boring, who had just been given a clean bill of health and released from hospital that morning, sat ram rod straight in a gold damask, down-filled Queen Anne style wingback chair with walnut cabriole legs, his back against the wall and his eyes darting this way and that at every little sound. The Duchess paced the floor in front of the windows pausing now and then to look out across the lush green lawns at the deep, dark and foreboding forest beyond.

Benjamin reposing in an Eames chair unobtrusively contemplated his fellow detainees as he observed them from behind a copy of The Paladin. Something was nagging at his thoughts. There was something about one of his unlikely companions that he couldn't just quite put his finger on. As a rule he seemed to possess an innate ability to judge character.

He reckoned Ulysses Upman to be narcissistic with feelings of grandiosity and entitlement. A bully who intimidates others demonstrating a complete lack of regard for the feelings of others. He enjoys taking risks never admits his mistakes.

Dr. Boring, if that was his real name, was the poseur of the group and possessed a very intriguing personality. He possesses an exceptionally high IQ and the natural ability to manipulate people around him without any feeling of guilt or remorse. On the contrary it gives him intense satisfaction encouraging him to continue his manipulation to obtain whatever he wants with total disregard for those he manipulates.

Boring is very intuitive about the weaknesses and insecurities of others and he knows how to match your interests. An eclectic consumer of information he can completely convince you he is an expert in the area of your interest. A photographic memory and an incredible memory for lies allows him to keep his stories straight.

In short, the Professor is a sociopath.

Turning his attention to the woman of mystery, Duchess Cassandra, he was conflicted. Although her personality was charming even to the point of being disarming her expression of emotions seemed to be mimicked and perhaps even mocking. She was meticulous down to the tiniest detail in everything she did.

Benjamin's contemplation was interrupted by Jarvis entering the drawing room pushing a tea trolley laden with raisin scones and fairy cakes and of course tea. "Jarvis, you truly are a Godsend." exclaimed Benjamin.

"Thank you sir. Will there be anything else?"

"No, thank you Jarvis. This is very timely, indeed.

I'll play mother, shall I?" Cassandra offered, repositioning the tea things to a more efficient arrangement. She poured four cups of the steaming liquor adding cream and sugar to order and then passing them around.

Everyone helped themselves to the pastries. This seemed a much needed respite from the tension in the room.

The Duchess strolled back to the windows repositioning crystal candle holders and Royal Dolton figures in a symmetrical arrangement on the mantle as she passed. Reaching the windows she caught sight of curious activity among the police officers on sentry duty. One of the constables received a radio communication and he motioned to a WPC and the pair walked quickly into Monks Hall.

A few moments later the pair of P. C. plods appeared but this time they had a prisoner in handcuffs between them. She couldn't believe her eyes. It was her sister, Cornett. They put her in the back seat of the Panda car and drove off.

It wasn't long before there was a flurry of activity outside and all of the Bizzies left the grounds except one outside their window. What was going on? Something had happened, but what?

She had to find out. She hurried from the room before anyone could enquire as to where she was going and why. Ulysses and Boring looked at one another questioningly and then they both looked at Benjamin who just shrugged.

Duchess Cassandra burst into the study demanding to know what was happening. "Where are you taking my sister and why was she in handcuffs?" she shrieked.

Logan looked up from the desk taken by surprise suddenly twigging on to what the Duchess had just blurted out. "Steady on! Did you say your sister? Well I'll be gobsmacked. I thought there was something very familiar about her. So, you are Chrystal D. Canter. Why didn't you say so earlier?"

"You didn't ask and I didn't think it was any of your business."

"We will need a DNA sample from you, Duchess."

"Now wait just one moment. What right do you have to demand such a thing? You can't possibly suspect that I had anything to do with any of this, surely." she loudly protested.

"This is a murder enquiry, Duchess, and that gives me not only the right but the duty. Now, you can either provide it voluntarily or I can take you down to the police station and we can do it there." Logan declared as he reached in the evidence kit and withdrew a sterile swab to take the DNA sample. "Open wide if you please, Duchess." directed Logan.

"Where have you taken my sister?" Duchess Cassandra demanded opening her mouth resignedly for the swab.

"She was being detained for further questioning in the murder of Sebastian Monk, Earl of Uppington on the Downs."

"What possible motive would she have? We haven't seen him for years.

Why all the commotion? What's happened? Has there been an accident?"

"Your sister has escaped. Now why would she do that if she had nothing to hide? She won't get far. I have a search party scouring Monks Wood and the surrounding area for her as we speak." DCI Wisdom replied sheepishly.

"But how? I saw her put in a car with two constables."

"When did you last see your sister?"

"We haven't seen each other for two or three years now. We were like chalk and cheese after Alvaro was murdered and our mother left us. I attended Oxford where I met Cob... rather, Clarence, Duke of Camelot.

What do you think you have against my sister? I'll engage the best team of Barristers and Solicitors."

"I would like your permission to search your suite, Duchess." DCI Wisdom requested respectfully.

"Whatever for? You have no right to invade my privacy. How dare you treat me like a common criminal."

"I reiterate, Duchess, this is a murder investigation and that not only gives me the authority but the duty to investigate every potential avenue of information. Having said that, I can seal your room until I obtain a search warrant if you would prefer."

"Very well, if you insist. I will be lodging my complaint with the Commissioner of Police of the Metropolis, Sir Robert Woodentop. Bobby is a close personal friend." she groused.

DCI Wisdom dismissed Duchess Cassandra, "We're finished for the moment, Duchess. You may return to the drawing room with your friends."

"They're barely acquaintances, hardly friends." the Duchess whinged.

Logan left the Duchess at the drawing room door and continued upstairs to her suite to begin his search. Opening the heavy oak door his senses were met with the smells of wood, wood polish, the pleasant whiff of burnt match sticks from the coal in her fireplace, and Chanel No. 5. A mahogany four poster bed was the central focus of the sleeping chamber accompanied by a 19th century mahogany chest of drawers all enclosed by four walls adorned with sumptuous William Morris pure Lodden wallpaper of brown and gold floral pattern on charcoal. A 19th century mahogany inlaid writing desk occupied an alcove and a small sitting area in the corner of the room was furnished with a pair of oval back mahogany chairs, an oval burl walnut tilt top coffee table and underfoot a hand knotted Persian Heriz oriental rug of blue and gold.

Forty five minutes later and having found nothing of interest, save for her penchant fastidiousness, he returned to the study to find Bartholomew Tussilago painstakingly examining the desk and Bailey quietly watching with contemplative interest.

"Oh, hello Bailey. What's he doing boy?" Logan asked as he scratched Bailey behind both ears.

"Discovery consists of seeing what everybody has seen and thinking what nobody has thought." Bailey thought at Logan in response.

Bat was deep in thought scrutinizing the Earl's antique Victorian burr walnut pedestal desk with an inset green gilt, hand tooled leather writing surface. The mahogany lined drawers looked magnificent with their gleaming polished brass drawer pulls and escutcheons.

Bat placed his hands on the edge of the desk and pushed lightly with his index fingers. There was a faint click and as if by magic a drawer that had hitherto been hidden popped open. All of a sudden a barely audible lilting melodic trilling could be heard all around them and then it was gone just as suddenly.

Looking in the tiny secret drawer what the two men saw took Logan's breath away. "Diamonds!" he whispered. "But how... The drawer... How did you know about the drawer?"

"It's a puzzle desk. I suspected it when I recognised it as an original Cab Netmaker design." Bat moved around the desk and sitting in the chair. He pulled out the centre drawer. His hand disappeared into the cavity, there was a barely discernible click and instantly another unseen chamber opened. It too was full of precious stones.

Bat removed one of the carbon crystals and examined it closely. A melodic trilling seemed to emanate from everywhere but before you could actually be sure of what you were hearing it came to an abrupt end.

Logan took one look blurting out, "Diamonds? What was he doing filling these hidey holes with all those diamonds? Why not keep them in a safe deposit box?"

"These are not just any diamonds my friend. The hardest substance known to man. A sign of wealth and fortune. Kings and Queens have worn these forms of concentrated carbon and countless millions have lusted after them. Diamonds!"

"Blimey! I'll be gobsmacked. There must be millions of pounds worth of ice here."

"Yes, Logan and very nasty they are too. Unless I miss my guess, you're looking at blood diamonds, a term used to describe a diamond mined in a war zone and sold to finance insurgency. These diamonds could have come from Angola, Ivory Coast, Sierra Leone, Democratic Republic of Congo, Republic of Congo or Liberia. These are all areas of conflict that the warlords are using diamonds to fund heinous crimes against humanity.

The United Nations has placed embargos on conflict diamonds.

After two years of negotiation between governments, diamond producers and non-government organizations a means of identifying conflict free diamonds, the Kimberley Process Certification Scheme was created. This system tracks diamonds from the mine to the market. We've been trying to track and apprehend the masterminds behind a blood diamond trafficking organization for months.

The trail lead us from an enigmatic and deadly warlord, Miss Teak, a diminutive and inscrutable oriental woman highly skilled in mysterious martial arts said to be headquartered in Sierra Leone to Picov Andropov. He had been using his shipping firm and connections to transport blood diamonds from Miss Teak to a shadowy syndicate here in the UK for laundering.

Then our investigations lead us to Sebastian Monk but both were murdered before we could learn who was actually running the organization."

Bat continued to examine the desk but could not find any more secret drawers.

Logan gathered all of the diamonds into evidence bags and thanked Bat for his assistance.

17 ANOTHER PUZZLE PIECE

Something niggled like an itch he couldn't quite reach at the back of Logan's mind as he sat in quiet contemplation of the most recent revelations. He pondered the lengths people went to keep secrets and conceal things and then it struck him. The papers found hidden in the Blue Boy painting were still in his pocket. Removing the evidence bag and donning a pair of latex gloves he carefully slid the papers from the manila evidence envelope.

He scanned the documents that had been concealed within the painting and encountered another surprising discovery. There was a Birth Certificate, Death Certificate and pathology report in the envelope. The Birth Certificate listed Sebastian Monk and one, Sue Vlaki, the estranged wife of a local Turkish businessman known to have ties to the Turkish mafia as the parents of an illegitimate male child. The document certified the birth of Charles Igor Phineas Monk.

The Death Certificate had been issued for a Sue Vlaki and cause of death was listed as drowning ruled a misadventure diving in Loch Ness in search of Nessie by the Coroner.

Finally, he read the pathology report on Sue Vlaki's autopsy which listed chlorine as one of the chemicals found in her lungs. Not what one would expect if she drowned in Loch Ness. Very suspicious indeed.

While Logan considered what the ramifications would be of these documents coming to light Sergeant B. Goodman entered the study breaking his train of thought.

"The search teams are completing their first sweep of the wood and I've sent a team into the secret passages. There has been no sign of the escaped prisoner Guv'nor."

"Good Sergeant. Keep me posted on the progress of the search." Logan directed.

The Sergeant's attention was drawn to the documents on the desk. "Cor, where did you find these? I never heard of a murder case involving a Sue Vlaki. It seems to me that chlorine in the lungs of a women supposedly drowned in a lake would raise a few questions."

"Yes, Sergeant. I want you to look into everything you can find on Sue Vlaki's death and the circumstances surrounding it."

"Right you are, Guv."

"I had a visit from Bartholomew Tussilago this afternoon and he was able to reveal the two secret drawers you see open here." Logan explained as he placed the evidence bags full of blood diamonds on the desk before the Sergeant. "These were found in the compartments.

I've informed the International Criminal Court (ICC) in the Hague and they're sending someone to retrieve them."

"Are they what I think they are, Guv?"

"Well Sergeant that depends on whether or not you think they are uncut diamonds."

"There must be millions of pounds worth there, Guv." the Sergeant said letting out a low whistle.

"We had a case a while back involving a few rough diamonds someone had used to pay a gambling debt. Turns out they were what they call blood diamonds."

"Who passed the diamonds?" asked DCI Wisdom.

"The bookie kept schtum. We couldn't shake him so we never found out, Guv."

"I must find the key to Sebastian's code. It must involve blackmail and blood diamonds. Was he the mastermind? Who tried to poison Countess Vera Lee Isay Monk and why?" Logan thought out loud.

"We need to speak with the Earl's guests again, I think, Sergeant. Please bring the Duchess first."

"Right you are, Guv."

It was late afternoon when Sergeant B. Goodman entered the drawing room to interview the guests. "Beg pardon, Duchess and gentlemen. We have a few more questions for you. Would you please come with me Duchess?"

"What does that P. C. Plod want with us now?" Ulysses groused.

Duchess Cassandra rose from her seat by the window and followed the Sergeant out of the drawing room.

"You wanted to see me DCI Wisdom?" the Duchess said coyly.

"Good Afternoon Duchess. Were you aware that the Earl was blackmailing your sister?"

The Duchess appeared to be strangely relieved when he asked her about her sister. "Please call me Cassandra.

I had no idea. What could he possibly have against her?"

"I came across the Earl's personal planner with several puzzling entries that caught my attention, Friday: 10:00 (1) CK; Saturday: 10:00 (2) LK; 11:00 (3) DK; 16:30 (4) CK; 13:00 (5) LK; Sunday: 11:30 (M) X. The number(2) refers to your sister, Cornett. I know that your sister, Cornett, is number (2), which one are you, Duchess?" he asked hoping to catch her off guard.

"W... why? Whatever do you mean, 'which one am I'? Surely you can't think that I'd be on that list?" she replied indignantly.

"Hmm. Let me see. I think you were (4). Arriving just ahead of Benjamin Wolf. That would mean your tribute was One hundred thousand British pounds in uncut blood diamonds. What was he holding over you, I wonder, Duchess Cassandra?"

She was very good at veiling her emotions but she couldn't conceal all of her reactions from Logan. He observed her eye brows flinch ever so slightly and he glimpsed fear flash in her eyes at his mention of blood diamonds.

"Nothing! He wasn't holding anything over me. You've got nothing but pure supposition, Detective Chief Inspector Wisdom.

I'll be leaving in the morning. I've had more than enough of this. We've all tolerated your whims long enough. Now if there's nothing else..."

"You have never been a prisoner here, Duchess. We won't be able to protect you if you leave but that certainly is your prerogative. You are free to leave at any time. Please leave an address and phone number where you may be reached with my Sergeant before you go."

He knew it was imperative he find the key to the Earl's code.

He evaluated the personalities of the remaining members of the group looking for the weakest link. "Escort the Duchess back to her friends and bring Mr. Upman back for questioning, Sergeant."

"Yes, Guv. After you, Duchess." he rumbled.

Within a few minutes the Sergeant was back with an inebriated real estate mogul.

"Good afternoon Mr. Upman. I won't keep you long. I just have one or two questions."

"Why aren't you out there looking for the fiend before another one of us is murdered?" he slurred.

"I assure you we are doing everything possible to apprehend the miscreant while keeping you safe. However, we can't guarantee your safety once you leave here.

Now then, we know that the Earl was blackmailing you and that you were to meet with him this weekend to make a payment. We also know you were to make that payment in blood diamonds. What time were you to make this payment, Mr. Upman?"

"H... how did you kn... know? I h... had nothing to do with his d... death." he whined panic beginning to rise.

"What time, Mr. Upman." Logan bellowed impatiently.

"R...r...right after lunch. A...about one o'clock. I had nothing to do with his death. I know how this looks but you must believe me. I paid him fifty thousand in diamonds and left him very much alive admiring the stones." Ulysses blubbered beginning to fall to pieces.

"What was his hold over you?"

Perspiration had broken out on his forehead and he was shaking as he whined, "I'll be ruined if word of this gets out. Is there any way we can keep this from the public?"

"We cannot promise anything but neither do we recklessly reveal confidential information. Now what was it that he held over you?"

"You have to understand, I was just starting my career and I was under tremendous pressure. It was a gigantic shopping mall project. I was facing bankruptcy someone came to me with an offer I couldn't refuse. It was like throwing a life preserver to a drowning man. Do you understand? I had to accept their offer." Ulysses boozily slurred through his tears.

"That will be all for now Mr. Upman. We'll talk again when you've had time to rest.

Sergeant take Mr. Upman up to his room and see that he gets to bed and then fetch Mr. Wolf for a few questions."

"Right you are sir."

After pouring Ulysses into his bed he went to the drawing room, "Would you come with me, please, Mr. Wolf, sir." said the Sergeant.

Rising from the comfort of the Eames chair he had been occupying he said, "Lead on Sergeant."

Pieces were beginning to fall into place but he still needed Sebastian's key to his code. His contemplation was interrupted by Sergeant Goodman entering the study. "Beg pardon, Guv, Mr. Wolf as you requested, sir."

The Sergeant went next door to the library to run a computer check on Sue Vlaki. Within twenty minutes he had learned that all the files pertaining to Sue Vlaki and her estranged husband, Vlad, had been mysteriously sealed with no further explanation. What he had been able to retrieve had been seriously redacted.

He rejoined DCI Wisdom and Benjamin Wolf in the study placing a report on the desk in front of DCI Wisdom. Logan opened the file to find several photos of Sue Vlaki and was frustrated to find the amount of redaction. He did notice, however, the mention of alkaloids in her blood.

One small detail he did notice though was a minuscule mark on her ankle. Could it be? He had to know. Getting the magnifying glass out of the desk drawer and peering at the photo he recognised the tiny tattoo of a Wormwood Star.

18 A GOODMAN GOES TO BATTLE

Logan knew he had to find Sebastian's code book and the leverage he had been holding over his victims. His eyes searched every inch of the room again but could see nothing out of the ordinary. He left the study and entered the library walking slowly around the perimeter examining the books, shelves, paintings as he moved. He found nothing unusual.

He stood in the fading light of the rapidly aging day trying to get into the mind of Sebastian Monk. Where would he keep his most valued possession? He would keep it somewhere close by and somewhere safe from prying eyes. Returning to the study deep in thought, Logan sat down in the chair behind the desk and looked around at every nook and cranny within arm's length. He reached absent mindedly for a snifter and decanter of Sebastian's favourite tipple, a fine brandy kept within easy reach on the credenza just as Sergeant Goodman entered followed by Benjamin Wolf. "Ah, good afternoon Mr. Wolf" he said his hand returning empty to the arm of his chair.

He stretched to the bell pull but before he could summon Jarvis he was in the doorway asking if he could be of service. Logan asked the disconcertingly efficient butler to bring them some tea.

"Yes sir." replied the servant, turning and disappearing without making a sound.

"Mr. Wolf."

"Please call me Ben."

"Ben, you knew the deceased well?"

"Yes, as well as anyone I suppose."

"Where do you think the Earl would hide something very important to him that he might want to access at a moment's notice?"

Ben closed his eyes in thought and touching his finger tips together he placed his hands together beneath his nose as if in prayer. A minute later he opened his eyes and rising from his chair in front of the desk strode to the credenza. Removing the drinks tray containing the brandy decanter and snifters he examined the surface of the wall behind. Then pressing his index finger on what appeared to be a knot in the wood and releasing a circular disk.

The level of anticipation rose dramatically in the room.

Underneath the disk they found a small keyhole. Logan quickly retrieved the mystery key from his pocket and inserting it into the lock turned it. A barely audible click was heard. He thought, at last, I'm going to find the illusive code book. Then opening the small door they were all excited to set eyes on a safe adorned with a triskelion, however, disappointment soon replaced their excitement when they saw the combination lock.

With quiet assurance Benjamin moved closer and slowly, delicately he turned the dial feeling, almost sensing for the tumblers to fall into place with each number of the combination. The DCI and the Sergeant stood mesmerized as the Illusionist methodically worked his way through the combination noting the numbers as he did so. Within five minutes he announced that the combination had been completed and stepped aside for DCI Wisdom to do the official honours.

"Well bless my soul. That was amazing, Mr. Wolf, sir." exclaimed the burly Sergeant.

"Thank you very kindly Ben. I would have had to call in forensics with their safe cracking team and equipment. It would have been hours before we'd have gotten into the safe. You have a remarkable talent." Logan exclaimed as he opened the safe revealing the code book and a flash drive.

Opening his laptop he plugged in the flash drive, "Hmmm. There are several files each labelled with a different person's name and number. The first five files were on Picov Andropov numbered (1), Cornett D. Canter (2), Dr. Isidore Marion Boring (3), Duchess Cassandra Webb (4), Ulysses Upman (5) and there were many more each named and numbered.

There's an accounting journal and ledger showing several sources of capital accumulation one of which is extortion and all of the capital is flowing through to numerous offshore accounts. I'll turn this over to forensic accounting for a complete clarification."

Logan had also noted a black, hand tooled leather bound diary of sorts, displaying a trinacrium[28] in the centre of its cover among the things in the safe, in which Sebastian mentioned his fear of someone he called the Chameleon and an organization called Rosa Ordo of the Manu Tenebris (R.O.M.T.) or Secret Order of the Hand of Darkness. He went on to describe how the Chameleon was, in fact, the Grand Poobah of the Triumvirate and it was whispered he or she possessed mystical powers.

"You haven't heard of something called the Rosa Ordo of the Manu Tenebris or R.O.M.T. by any chance?" he asked Ben broodingly.

"Yes, I have. Are they involved in this somehow?" Ben asked apprehensively.

"I don't know for sure, Ben, but it looks like they could be. Sebastian's diary mentions the R.O.M.T. and someone called the Chameleon."

"They are a distinctly malevolent and enigmatic organization, if they even exist at all. The tales are all anecdotal steeped in myth and legend. But if the yarns are even to be half believed they will be a very nasty foe indeed."

---

[28] star with three points from trinacria meaning triangle referring to the shape of the island of Sicily

"Thanks again Ben. I'd like you to return to the others and I'd appreciate your observations."

"My pleasure, Logan." Ben agreed as he rose to leave.

"Sergeant please bring Duchess Cassandra Webb in for further questions."

"Right you are Guv'nor." agreed the amiable Sergeant.

Entering the drawing room Sergeant B. Goodman looked around but there was no sign of the Duchess. Addressing the doctor he asked, "Where has the Duchess gone, Dr. Boring?"

"Why... I... have no idea, Sergeant. I... haven't taken much notice for a while. I've been reading trying to forget about the bizarre and terrifying goings on."

"I see." said the Sergeant as he turned and left the room to go in search of the Duchess. The foyer was cold and dimly lit. Circling a round table occupying the centre of the foyer, inlaid with two diverse woods of different tones creating a star with an ebony veneer ring a base heavily carved around a black obsidian sphere atop claw feet the Sergeant mounted the staircase. Climbing to the hall above he turned towards the front of the house and quickly made his way to the Duchess' room. He knocked on her door but got no response. He tried again with no answer. Opening the door to her room he found it empty but in a state of disarray as if she packed in a hurry. Moving slowly around the room he noticed that the mahogany wardrobe with its hand carved ornate doors was slightly out of place as if someone had been looking for something behind it. Reaching behind the wardrobe he could feel a draft of cool air coming from the gap.

Pulling on the cabinet it swung into the room easily on its hinges revealing a gaping doorway into darkness.

Rushing out of the room, down the stairs, around the table and out the front door he found her car hadn't been moved. Approaching the vehicle he became subconsciously aware of the symbol, a trinacrium or Wormwood Star, affixed to the bonnet. Without hesitation he lifted the bonnet and disconnected the ignition wires.

Next he went back to the study to report to DCI Wisdom regarding the missing Duchess.

Before Logan could say, "put a search team together," they heard a thunderous commotion in the drawing room. Losing no time the two men rushed to the source of the fracas. Without warning and just as they glimpsed what appeared to be two identical women locked in mortal combat they were plunged into the heart of darkness. The night was moonless, breathless and silent save for the din of battle raging in the inky blackness of the drawing room.

"C'mon Sergeant. We've got to get in there." shouted Logan.

"I can't see a thing, Guv'nor but right you are." he yelled. Then bellowing, "BUAIDH NO BÀS!" (Victory or death!) like a thundering bull gone mad the big man charged into the room.

There was a hullabaloo of blood curdling screams, breaking furniture, then there was what sounded like raw meat being pulverized, and finally groans and moans. Logan apprehensively shown his electric torch about the room searching for his Sergeant. The light from his torch moved over splintered wood, bits and bobs of torn and shredded unrecognizable material and broken glass. The beam from the torch illuminated a scene of destruction. Then he saw something moving on the far side of the room and as his eyes adjusted to the dust and gloom he could see Sergeant B. Goodman pinning down two females. One of the culprits was the Duchess and the other her doppelganger but which one was the Duchess? The pair silently glowered at the Sergeant and each other.

"Alright Sergeant?" enquired DCI Wisdom.

He looked like he had just emerged from a fight with two cats in a blender. His sleeve was torn asunder revealing rivulets of blood running down a well muscled arm. There was a dark patch on his tunic where a pocket should have been and his helmet was missing. He sported a nasty looking mouse under his left eye that would soon become a purple and green battle badge of honour.

"Yes, Sir, Guv'nor. If you could just lend a hand with the handcuffs, Guv, I'd be most grateful." said a much dishevelled Sergeant.

After they had appropriately restrained the two she-devils they began to sift through the rubble for any sign of Dr. Boring. There was evidence of a bloody battle. Logan feared the worst for Isidore.

All of a sudden they were blinded when the lights unexpectedly came back on. Within a few moments the men had recovered their sight and then they heard a groan coming from under the overturned settee. The men rushed to each end of the chesterfield quickly flipping it back to its upright position and underneath they found a battered and dazed Dr. I. M. Boring.

"Alright Doctor?" enquired Logan.

"I... I think so. My throat is burning and my head is splitting." he moaned. Reaching his hand to his throat he felt something warm and sticky. Looking down at his hand he discovered it was covered with blood and abruptly he fainted.

Logan put in a call for an ambulance and then he looked around expecting to see the constable they had left on sentry duty. Picking up his radio he called the sentry with no response. He then called the team leader of the search party to call off the search and return to Monks Hall and went in search of the sentry saying to Sergeant Goodman, "Stay here Sergeant. I'm going to look for the Constable on duty."

"Yes, Guv'nor." he replied with foreboding.

Logan charged outside to the sentry's designated position to find the unconscious figure of the Constable shoved, unceremoniously beneath some shrubs next to the French doors leading from the drawing room. Helping the Constable into a sitting position he asked the groggy man, "What happened Constable? Who did this to you?"

Not able to get a coherent response from the man he waited for the paramedics to arrive. Within a few minutes the search team arrived anticipating new orders.

"I need two Constables with me. The rest of you deploy yourselves about the grounds around the house and stay in sight of each other at all times."

"Yes, Guv'nor." replied the team leader.

Looking up the drive he spotted the paramedics arriving. After the paramedics checked over and stabilized the incapacitated officer for transport to the hospital they gave details of their diagnosis to the D.C.I. He had been throttled into unconsciousness from behind and he should make a full recovery and probably released later that day. As they bundled the Constable onto the gurney for transport but before they loaded him onto the ambulance he motioned to Wisdom to come closer. The D.C.I. leaned near enough to hear the Constable hoarsely whisper, "I'm sorry Guv'nor."

"It could have happened to the best of us, Constable. Do you remember anything that could help us apprehend your assailant?"

"I... I remember smelling perfume a... and I'm certain it was a woman's arm around my throat, Guv'nor."

"You've been very helpful, Constable. Now you just concentrate on recovering.

There are other casualties inside for you to check out. Come with us." The two Constables and the paramedics followed Logan into the Hall to the battleground of the drawing room where he instructed the paramedics to see to Dr. I. M. Boring then examine the two women for possible injuries.

When the paramedics had tended to Isidore and completed their examination of the two vixens he instructed the Constables to take the two miscreants to the local constabulary where he would question them later.

The paramedics took Isi to the waiting ambulance then returned and busied themselves tending to the Sergeant, cleaning and binding his wounds. When they had finished Logan said, "Alright Sergeant?"

To which the amiable Sergeant stood up quickly, replying, "Right as rain, Guv." and then he immediately sat back down unceremoniously hard on the floor. "Sorry, Guv. Just stood up a little too quickly." he said with a sheepish look as he rose more slowly, dusting himself off.

"Go home Sergeant. Get cleaned up and put on a clean shirt and another tunic. Get yourself a cup o' splash. Then meet me at the station house to question the suspects.

19 THE MARK OF THE BEAST

Logan trudged across the front of Monks Hall, his comfortable black calf leather, classic brogues crunching in the gravel driveway with each step, to Countess Vera Lee Isay Monk's apartments. Passing the Venitia Z 200 again his attention was drawn back to the symbol of the Wormwood Star on the bonnet. His pace slowed as he began to make connections with Sebastian's diary, the tiny key with the triskelion and the sinister organization, the R.O.M.T.

Reaching the main entrance he crossed the polished marble foyer to her rooms in search of Lady Christine. Noticing, as he traversed the vestibule, the portrait of the Viscount had been removed from its place of veneration and now sat ignominiously on the floor against the wall. Then he spotted what looked like a birth mark on the boy's leg but when he looked closer he could just make out a small tattoo.

Cat met him in the doorway and greeted him with a kiss on the cheek making Logan blush and raising his spirits.

"I only have a few minutes. I just had to see for myself that you and your Aunt were safe and sound. How is your Aunt feeling?" asked Logan.

"Aunt Vera Lee is feeling much better. What were you looking at?"

"I don't know. Perhaps nothing. Why is this painting out here in the entry hall?"

"It's going to an art restorer to see if it can be repaired."

"Would your Aunt have a magnifying glass?"

"Wait a minute I'll see." She was back almost immediately with a hand held lens handing it to Logan.

He picked up the portrait and placed it on the hall table and taking the glass from Cat he bent closer examining the mark on the boy's calf. Focusing the glass he exclaimed, "Hello, what's this, then?" He handed the glass to Cat.

"Well I'll be. What does it mean, Logan?"

"It's a Wormwood Star, Cat. That's the sign of the R.O.M.T. It's too much to be a coincidence. I've found the same symbol to be the emblem on Duchess Cassandra's Venitia Z 200, a small key I found in Earl's pocket, his wall safe and on his diary. What do you make of that, Cat?"

"I think we need to talk to Bartholomew as soon as possible." urged Lady Christine.

"I've got to meet Sergeant Goodman at the station house to interview Duchess Cassandra and Cornett D. Canter about their involvement in recent events just now. Would you arrange a meeting with Bat?" but before he could take his leave Bat entered the sitting room from the Countess Vera Lee Isay Monk's bedroom.

"Don't get sidetracked from your core investigation Logan. There are connections with the R.O.M.T. and they will need to be dealt with but follow the family history. That's where you will find your motives the R.O.M.T. connections will only be background noise in your case." counselled the Paladin.

"Thank you Bat. Now I best be getting to the police station to question two nasty pieces of work."

"Call me when you can Logan." exhorted Lady Christine earnestly.

Logan nodded agreement saying, "Goodnight you two." to Cat and Bat. He left feeling chuffed to bits.

The Station House came into view and it occurred to Logan it was a rock in the shifting sands of life. A refuge to the abused and tormented, and a place of terror and internment to miscreants.

He tripped lightly up the Station House steps but could feel his mood of twitterpation dissolving as he climbed and by the time he entered the door of interrogation room one only a glimmer remained. He experienced an atmosphere of the immensity of the desperation of those who had passed through these interrogation rooms. Closing the door he sat down in the chair across the table from Cornett looking intently at her as if trying to see into her soul. He opened the file in front of him and turned on the interview recorder. "It's Thursday, September twenty-eighth 18:17. In attendance are Sergeant B. Goodman and Detective Chief Inspector Logan Wisdom interviewing Miss Cornett D. Canter.

Let's start at the beginning, shall we. What were you and the Duchess fighting about?"

"Nothing." she groused.

"Come now, Miss Canter, surely you can't expect me to believe that."

"We'll pay for any damage and make our apologies to the Viscount and Countess. I'm sure they will understand. Have they pressed charges?"

"This is a multiple homicide investigation, Miss Canter. It requires your full cooperation." he stated flatly.

"Let me tell you what we know.

We know, for instance, that you and Duchess Cassandra, or should I say Chrystal D. Canter, are twin sisters. We also know that your biological parents are Brandy D. Canter and Sebastian Monk, Earl of Uppington on the Downs.

Were you fond of your parents?"

"Of course. What are you trying to get at?"

"Your mother had a restraining order against your father and then filed for divorce. He must have been a very violent man. Did he ever mistreat you or your sister?"

"No! He loved me. He wanted to protect us and teach us. Mother couldn't understand that. She turned her back on Daddy and took us away, destroying our family."

"We are aware that your step father, Alvaro Canter, was murdered and your mother is missing. We also know that your step father was poisoned with alkaloids distilled from the Datura plant and then garrotted. It seems there has been a lot of that going around lately.

You attended assassin training as a member of The Assassins Society at Durham University didn't you? And I see here you became extremely proficient in the use of the garrotte."

"All you have is circumstantial. It won't stand up in a court of law." she spat back.

"We have your DNA on both the knife used to stab Sebastian Monk and the garrotte with which he was throttled. What I don't understand is why you poisoned him first." He was met with silence.

"Were you aware that Sebastian was already dead when you garrotted him?"

Again he was met with silence but this time he thought he saw surprise and disbelief pass fleetingly across her face.

He persisted, "We also know that both you and Chrystal underwent psychoanalysis and furthermore we know your attending physician was Dr. E. Ville, Chartered Clinical Psychologist, AKA Dr. I. M. Boring, AKA Abacas Beancounter.

At some point you discovered that Dr. E. Ville was a fraud. How did that make you feel?"

"Chrystal wanted to k... quit, just cancel our sessions and report him. I never believed we needed anybody's help in the first place."

"Had your sister discovered you were the murderer and was she trying to stop you from killing again?"

"No, I told you I had nothing to do with the murders." with that she crossed her arms and gave Logan a murderous look.

There was a knock at the door and Sergeant Goodman poked his head in announcing, "The other sister, Chrystal, would like to speak with you, Guv."

DCI Wisdom nodded to the Sergeant and rose from his chair saying, "Thank you Sergeant. This may be your last chance to tell your side of the story." Silence.

"I need a coffee. I'll be back to see if you've changed your mind before I speak with your sister. DCI Wisdom terminating the interview Thursday at 18:35." he said as he switched off the recording device. Logan left the room leaving Cornett to fret over what her sister might be telling him. A chain is only as strong as its weakest link and Logan believed that instead of having a close relationship with her sister she had no capacity for love. She lacks remorse, shame or guilt and would not hesitate to throw her sister to the wolves if she believed it would be in her own best interest.

He entered the neighbouring interview room coffee in hand to observe Cornett through the one way glass as she paced the floor and bit her nails Then she appeared to come to a conclusion as she returned to her chair and calmly waited for him to come back. This could be the break he was waiting for or she could have guessed what he was doing. He waited another few minutes before going back in and as he watched she again became agitated and it was then he re-entered the room. This time he was accompanied by Sergeant Goodman.

Turning on the recording machine he began, ""It's Thursday at 18:45 and this is DCI Wisdom accompanied by Sergeant B. Goodman interviewing Miss Cornett D. Canter.

Well, are you going down for the murders alone or do I see what Chrystal has to say?"

Tears began rolling down her cheeks and she began to tremble, turning on every emotional ploy she had, as she spoke, "I'm so sorry Detective Chief Inspector. I never meant for things to get out of hand this way.

I only meant to give Sebastian what he demanded and leave but that wasn't enough for him. He put his hands on me. His own daughter! Before I could stop myself the karambit[29] was in my hand and I lashed out. The next thing I remember was coming to covered in dirt and leaves in a shallow grave in the Monks Wood.

I was in shock and something must have snapped inside me when he buried me alive. Everything was a blur and I don't remember much.

I had nothing to do with any of the other murders. It was Chrystal. You must believe me."

Without saying a word to the woman he switched off the recorder saying, "DCI Wisdom terminating the interview at 18:53." and rose to leave.

"Where are you going? You believe me don't you?"

He turned to Sergeant Goodman saying, "Sergeant, escort Miss Canter to her cell."

"Wait, you can't just leave. Say something."

Meanwhile, Chrystal had been impatiently walking about the room muttering to herself, anyone and no one her irritation. Logan stood in the adjacent room observing through the one way glass. As he watched she unconsciously flipped her hair and it was then he spotted it. A tiny tattoo at the base of her neck beneath her hair, a wormwood star. What did it mean? Was it the mark of the beast or a simple fad? Was she part of a conspiracy or was she acting alone?

Logan entered the room as Chrystal turned to face him with a smile of disarmingly angelic innocence and her emerald green eyes flashing. "Where have you been, Detective Chief Inspector Wisdom? I've been waiting for you." The sensation of evil menace was electrifying.

Logan took the seat at the table opposite Chrystal placing a file folder on the table in front of him. Switching the recorder on he stated for the record, " It's Thursday, September twenty-eighth 19:12. In attendance are Constable

---

[29] This knife, especially useful in self-defence, is so old no one is sure where it came from. The grip rests n the hand so perfectly that it is very difficult to disarm anyone holding one.

Lou Tennant and Detective Chief Inspector Logan Wisdom interviewing Duchess Cassandra Webb, AKA Chrystal D. Canter.

What were you and your sister fighting about?"

"You get right to the point, DCI Wisdom. No small talk?

I like that so if you must know Cornett was upset because I tried to end her miserable life."

"Why did you want to kill your sister?" Logan asked incredulously.

"Somehow she found out that I had dispatched our mother and that I had attempted to kill her love interest." she said wryly.

"And just who might her love interest be and why did you want to kill him?"

"Abacas Beancounter. You know him as Dr. I. M. Boring. He once tried to psychoanalyse us in his persona as Dr. E. Ville. He's nothing but a sociopathic buffoon. I have no idea what she sees in that inferior specimen of a human."

"You have been very busy. Why did you kill Mrs. Sue Vlaki?" he asked abruptly and catching her off guard..

"Her husband, Vlad, put out a contract on her which suited my purpose."

"You mean because she had seduced your father and they had a child together, your half brother the Viscount Charles Monk?"

"I wanted to kill him too because father didn't even acknowledge I existed."

"Where were you on Friday afternoon between the hours of 13:00 and 15:00?"

"I was indulging in a delicious lunch of whitebait and dill mayo with a sliced fennel, orange and almond salad accompanied by a very nice Muscadet-Sur-Lie in the quaint little village of Rolling Downs. I saw Benjamin Wolf there but he didn't even notice me." she purred with a sly sneer.

Logan decided to take the direct approach, "Why did you kill Picov Andropov?"

"Because that was my directive." was all she said.

"Who do you take orders from, Chrystal?"

"I take orders from no one. I am a Duchess and I'll thank you to remember that, Detective Chief Inspector." she protested haughtily.

"Is there a significance to your tattoo of the Wormwood Star?"

"It's Cob's family crest.

Andropov had become a liability. Sebastian had learned of his connection to the R.O.M.T. and was blackmailing him so Sebastian had to be eliminated as well."

"Why did you attempt to kill the Countess Vera Lee Isay Monk? What threat did she pose?"

"That wasn't down to me. I've never met the woman.

I tire of this tedious tête-à-tête and your inane questions. I had hoped for a more interesting exchange of ideas. Instead our discourse has been rather one sided. You don't live up to your surname, D.C.I. Wisdom. Are all law enforcement plods intellects as inferior as yours?"

D.C.I. Wisdom smiled as he rose to leave. Reaching the door he turned as if he had just remembered something and asked, "Who is the Chameleon?"

Her cold, emotionless countenance experienced a sudden transformation. She appeared gripped by the icy hands of fear. He even thought he saw her tremble.

Instantly regaining her composure she said, "I'm sure I have no idea and if you have any sense you will pursue that subject no further. If you do you do so at your peril." With that she refused to go further so Logan terminated the interview and turned off the recorder.

Logan left the room instructing Constable Lou Tennant to escort the prisoner to the cells then go home and get some rest.

20 CHAMELEON

"Take no part in the unfruitful works of darkness, but instead expose them." Ephesians 5:11

It was early the next morning as a delivery boy trotted down the steps from the Countess' apartment climbed onto his bicycle and peddled unobtrusively down the drive and out through the gates. Around a bend in the road and out of sight of the Hall he unexpectedly pulled off the road into a hidden lane and came to a stop. Dumping the bicycle in the bushes after wiping it clean of finger prints he knelt down and taking hold of the corner of a tarpaulin so well camouflaged it would have been impossible to have seen it if you had been standing next to it. Returning to a standing position he deftly and swiftly peeled the cover from his waiting Venitia Stealth Avenger motorcycle. Climbing into the saddle he pushed the starter button the quiet yet powerful electric motor whirred to life.

Turning the throttle the Avenger surged forward. He sped silently through the forest. The specially designed dual purpose tires gripped the forest floor of wet leaves like the claws of a jungle cat and he negotiated the woodland obstacles of rocks, logs, gullies and ridges. The rider was blissfully unaware, as he focused on skilfully manoeuvring his two wheeled steed cross country, of the eyes that had followed him since leaving Monks Hall.

Skidding to an abrupt halt just before he broke free of the concealment of the deep, dark wood. Reaching into his saddle bag he withdrew a dark bundle. He parked his ride beneath a tree covering it again with the camouflage tarp then removing his riding togs he quickly donned a police constable's uniform. He slung a leather pouch, exhibiting a small bulge, over his left shoulder and carried a small metal case in his right hand. Even his face had been transformed to that of a moustached older constable with greying hair.

He left his position of safety and strode confidently toward the station house only a short distance away. He entered the police station and went directly to the evidence lockup unchallenged, unlocked the door and within seconds located the evidence obtained from Sebastian Monk's study. He removed several containers and replaced them with what appeared to be identical containers. It would be hours perhaps days before the exchange was discovered.

Outside the evidence lockup he encountered Constable Lou Tenant. "You're new here. I'm glad I'm not the newest recruit in the precinct. Constable Lou Tenant." she said introducing herself and extending her hand.

"Constable Joe King. It's my pleasure I'm sure. Sorry, I can't chat now. They want me back at Monks Hall." replied the phony Constable King.

"Maybe we could have a coffee later and compare notes." offered Constable Tenant to her new acquaintance's receding back as he walked briskly down the corridor and out the station doors. He was chuffed that he had put one over on the slow witted P. C. Plod.

Returning to his Stealth Avenger he stood for a moment before replacing his police constable uniform with his stealth riding leathers and opened one of the packages and a self satisfied smile passed over his features as he reviewed the glittering contents. He stowed the uniform after removing the cover from his motorcycle then tucked the contraband into his saddle bags. He was uneasy as he looked around for anyone in the vicinity when he could find no one he straddled the machine, switched from electric motor to combustion engine, fired it up and set out for a rendezvous with the R.O.M.T. ruling council.

Though he saw no one nevertheless his every move was being watched. It had been observed that the rider had returned without the metal case. A magical trilling drifted briefly on the gentle breeze and then it was gone. There was a flash of motion and a figure appeared sprinting towards the station house. Approaching the desk sergeant Bat presented his credentials as a Paladin straight away. Next he directed the desk sergeant to evacuate the station house while he went in search of the explosive device he believed had been secreted somewhere in the building.

He immediately made for the station cafeteria located approximately in the centre of the structure and where a bomb would cause maximum destruction. He didn't search for long before he found the explosive. It was highly sophisticated but within three heart stopping minutes he had disarmed it. Disarming various complex explosive devices was part of his daily training regimen among other highly specialized physical, combat and mental exercises. He gave the all clear and instructed the desk sergeant to call the bomb squad to dispose of the device.

Before anyone could question him about how he knew there was a bomb he was gone. Fortunately he had had the forethought to place a tracking device on the Stealth Avenger. He mounted his own, specially designed high performance stealth motorcycle. Switching over from the solar powered 200 horse power electric motor with a top speed of 225 miles per hour to a turbocharged hybrid internal combustion power plant capable of running on propane, gasoline, diesel or just about any combustible liquid, putting out 320 horse power and a top speed of 300 miles per hour. He switched off the stealth cloaking that had veiled his motorcycle and switched on the onboard computer and it immediately lit up showing the exact location of his target. There was no time to lose the target was on the move. The Chameleon was headed for the clandestine lair of the infamous Secret Order of the Hand of Darkness or R.O.M.T. Their base of operations lay in a vaulted subterranean chamber hidden beneath the ruins of Cadaverous Castle. Built during the 13th century by Augusta Wind, nicknamed the Wizard of Chaos by the locals, believed to be a powerful warlock and carried out arcane rituals in the castle.

Bat knew that once the Chameleon met with the R.O.M.T. council he would go to ground to resurface where least expected. This would be the

Paladin's last opportunity to bring the enterprise of this extremely dangerous villain to an abrupt halt. However, he wanted to cut the head off of the serpent by capturing the members of the council. He called in a few old friends.

Bat called Jack Kettle, publican of The Bucket of Blood pub in the village of Coffinsrise, a big man standing six foot seven inches tall and as sturdy as an oak yet gentle as a lamb. Jack and Bat had collaborated in past adventures the latest adventure had been The Shadow Man.

His second invitation went out to Mynju Manners, his aging personal assistant and a retired Gurkha decorated by the Queen with the Conspicuous Gallantry Cross for single handedly vanquishing thirty enemy combatants that had had the temerity to attack a barracks of sleeping soldiers.

His final call went to Detective Chief Inspector Logan Wisdom of New Scotland Yard who said he would meet Bat at Cadaverous Castle with a squad of police officers.

21 DRAGON'S BREATH

The Paladin found a certain amount of comfort in knowing he had put together a consummate team. He turned his thoughts from his team to the Chameleon as he barrelled through Penrith to the outskirts where he would rendezvous with his Havoc armoured stealth helicopter containing his team members Jack and Mynju as they raced toward the Barony of Cadaverous in pursuit of the Chameleon.

After greetings of the comrades in arms the trio settled in for the brief journey to Cadaverous.

Upon reaching their destination they landed out of sight of the castle and alighted from the Havoc. Bat sent the Havoc away and would radio the pilot if needed. Approaching the castle from its blind side continually being vigilant for any signs of surveillance they sought places of concealment from which to keep watch until their quarry arrived.

Bat pressed the night scope to his eye and scanning the ruins he spotted several sentries. He dispatched Mynju to silently neutralize the sentinels. He then sent Jack to pose as the sentry closest to the entrance in case their target expected a guard to be on duty.

Mynju as silently as a breath incapacitated four of the five sentries but the fifth one had chanced upon what Mynju was doing. Fortunately Jack was within range. He grabbed the massive villain, who must have stood six foot four and sported a cauliflower ear, before the thug had time to raise the alarm or strike the little Ghurkha. Jack's huge pile driver fist caught the nasty piece of work beneath his jaw laying him out colder than a mackerel just in time to replace him at his post before his absence was noticed.

The day was overcast and damp with a chill in the air. Logan had stationed his squad of officers some distance away to avoid detection. He called Bat making him aware that backup had arrived and were in position.

It was at that moment Bat noticed fleeting movement at the entrance to the cavernous subterranean assembly hall. Making his way cautiously to the doorway He alerted Logan that their quarry was in the trap and motioned to his team to join him as he disappeared into the darkness. Within seconds he had made a rapid about face bellowing, "Bomb, get out! Bomb, get out!"

Jack and Mynju were hot on Bat's heels in retreat as the hot, bituminous wind, like a dragon's breath, propelled them along the blackened corridor. The trio plunged into the open as if spat from a beast's gaping maw. Logan and his men had not yet entered and when they saw Bat and his mates beating a hasty withdrawal they too judiciously took cover and just in the nick of time. There was an angry rumbling from deep within the bowels of the ruins as if they had awakened a sleeping beast. Followed by an ear splitting roar.

The air was instantly filled with choking dust and frenetically flying deadly high velocity missiles launched with a fury by the unfathomable demon. Flames of yellow and green shot skyward like tongues from the jaws of a mythological monster as they licked the air hungrily searching for something to devour.

Then it was over leaving everyone's ears ringing and eyes stinging from the choking dust cloud. Picking himself up off the ground, Jack checked to be sure Mynju was alright and looking around for Bat saw him sprinting at top speed towards another smoking hole some distance away and beyond he caught sight of a figure vanishing rapidly into the distance. There was something vaguely familiar about the diminutive form fading from sight but he couldn't quite put his finger on it.

Returning to the dumbfounded defenders of justice as they milled about dazed, Bat explained, "I had noticed the smoke emanating from what appeared to be an alternate means of egress from the smouldering abyss and glimpsed a figure running away. Unfortunately by the time I reached the exit the fleeing miscreant had gotten into a waiting automobile and made good his escape before I could reach him."

Bat approached a somewhat bewildered DCI Logan to alert him to the fact that the ICC would be sending a team to the scene and cooperation would be greatly appreciated.

22 A TINY ENIGMA

The landscape of the ancient castle ruin was one of utter devastation. What had been a site of historic significance had now been reduced to one of utter desolation. Not one stone stood atop another. Nearby trees had been stripped bare of their leaves and everything within a two hundred meter radius lay beneath a blanket of dust and rubble.

Logan and his squad set to work securing the scene to await the arrival of SOCO and the ICC. Logan had also called in a team of engineers to determine the safety of the last vestiges of the cavern and an excavator to ascertain if anyone had been entombed and if so to exhume their bodies.

The team of engineers with their construction crew and the excavator reopened the cavern making it safe for SOCO to enter. Hours later under the intense illumination of floodlights they could find no human remains to be taken back to the medical examiner's lab for identification. Any possible trace of what the hall had been used for by this clandestine group had been pulverized into fine powder.

The Chameleon had been tidying up loose ends.

Logan signalled his squad to wrap it up for the night when he was excitedly approached by a fresh recruit, Constable A. Kidd, holding a piece of paper in her hand. He took the fragment and examined it. It was the closing of a letter which read: "Sincerely, Miss Teak". "Well spotted Constable." praised the DCI which drew a broad, toothy grin from A. Kidd.

There was a shout from somewhere in the inky blackness of the tunnel and Logan made his way quickly to the location from which the call had come. Arriving he found Constable Tu Pritty holding the remnants of what appeared to be an ancient leather bound tome. Cleaning the grime from its surface revealed the vestiges of a black angel's wing and black sword.

"Good work Constable." commended DCI Wisdom. You couldn't see it in the darkness but the young Constable Tu Pritty's chest puffed out just a little bit and she stood ever so slightly taller with pride.

Well, at least they had evidence the Rosa Ordo of the Manu Tenebris (R.O.M.T.) or Secret Order of the Hand of Darkness had been conducting secret meetings in the hall.

The cold and damp night air combined with the fatigue of the day's events had left Logan feeling chilled to the bone and melancholy. They wrapped up finally around midnight.

Logan sat in a hot bath sipping a brandy and mulling over the case. The warmth was returning to his weary bones at long last as tiny wisps of steam rose from the hot water surrounding him. It was clear that Chrystal D. Canter also known as Her Grace Cassandra Webb, Duchess of Camelot, had murdered Sebastian Monk, Earl of Uppington on the Downs, her estranged and abusive father and her step-father Alvaro Canter. Furthermore she had attempted the murder of Countess Vera Lee Isay Monk who spawned their abuser. And lastly, the attempted murder of Isidore Abacas Beancounter also known as Isi Gil Tiornot, Barrister; Dr. E. Ville, Chartered Clinical Psychologist; and Dr. Daryl B. Payne, surgeon; and his latest incarnation Professor Isidore Marion Boring, Dr. of Philosophy because, not only was he a fraud but he knew her secret.

That leaves the murder of Picov Andropov, the transportation mogul, unaccounted for. Something nagged at him. Something he had witnessed. It was no use. The harder he tried the more elusive the puzzle piece became.

Cornett D. Canter would have to do some time in prison but he was sure that the extenuating circumstances of being buried alive and the family history of abuse by the Earl would predispose the court in her favour.

He climbed from the bath warmed through from tip to toe and ready for sleep. Just as his head hit the pillow his eyes flew open. He had it! Chrystal D. Canter had the same Wormwood Star tattoo that the Viscount had. They were both working for the R.O.M.T. It had been Chip that had tried to poison his Grandmother, not Chrystal.

Things were finally coming together but now he must get some much needed sleep. He wanted to be fresh for his rendezvous with Cat the next day. What was he saying it was the next day.

23 CORAM DEO[30]

"He saw that there was no man, and wondered that there was no one to intercede; then his own arm brought him salvation, and his righteousness upheld him. He put on righteousness as a breast plate, and a helmet of salvation on his head; he put on garments of vengeance for clothing, and wrapped himself in zeal as a cloak." Isaiah 59:16-17 ESV

The villain, Miss Teak, had made good her escape from the clutches of the long arm of the law, or so she thought. Fleeing down the motorway at top speed she watched as the scene of devastation rapidly vanished from sight in her rear view mirror.

Beside her on the seat was a briefcase and inside were blood diamonds worth millions of Euros. She had outwitted the slow witted Bizzies[31] and the R.O.M.T., foolish enough to think she was working for them. There was no one alive that had witnessed her true appearance as a result no one could identify her. She would ship the diamonds to her secret lair in Sierra Leone then get on the first plane out of England. She'd be home and dry, the

---

[30] a Latin phrase translated "in the presence of God" from Christian theology which summarizes the idea of Christians living in the presence of, under the authority of, and to the honour and glory of God.
[31] Police

English say, in thirty six hours.

Turning onto a side road that twisted and turned like the writhing of a serpent taking her ever higher through the ancient forest. The day was overcast with a light drizzle and the roadway was strewn with fallen leaves making the road she travelled as treacherous as riding a greased snake. She couldn't resist one more look. Opening the briefcase she was dumbfounded. A deafening blast from the horn of an oncoming lorry brought her attention sharply back to the road before her. Dazzling beams from giant headlamps blinded her. She applied the brake and turned the wheel to take evasive action and instantly her vehicle went spiralling out of control. All she saw before she blacked out was spinning flashes of lights, fence posts and trees.

She awoke chilled through, dazed and disorientated lying on a cold, hard concrete bed with a very thin mattress, covered with a gauze like blanket and surrounded by strange sounds and unpleasant odours. It wasn't until her eyes began to focus she became horribly aware of her surroundings. She was enclosed in a filthy room of no more than 1.8 metres (6 feet) by 2.5 metres (8 feet) of cement block walls covered in graffiti. The furnishings consisted of one hard wooden stool, a shelf affixed to the wall, a basin and a water closet.

Where was she and how had she gotten here? Her last memory was that of being blinded by bright lorry lights and spinning out of control. Then, in disbelief, she heard her name called through the cell bars. Three men stood outside her cell. One of the imposing male specimens of similar stature looking at her from the right side of the bars possessed lustrous silver hair and electric blue eyes, the other's unfathomable grey eyes were like swirling pools of mercury. The third man, the one that had called her name, had steel blue eyes and black hair, he was the copper.

"How are you feeling, Miss Teak? I'm DCI Logan Wisdom and you are under arrest for murder. You will be formally charged shortly but until then, You do not have to say anything. But it may harm your defence if you do not mention when questioned something which you later rely on in court. Anything you do say may be given in evidence.

Do you understand, Miss Teak?" asked Logan.

"Yes, yes. I understand.

Where am I? How did I get here and who are your friends, DCI Wisdom? Where's my lawyer?" she groused irritably.

"You are precisely where you belong, in prison. You ran your car off the road last night.

What did you do with the diamonds you took from the police evidence room? It might go a little easier for you if you tell us."

"I didn't do anything with them. I don't know how you did it but somehow they melted. Now, you have nothing to hold me on."

"We have plenty to hold you on. You will remain a guest of Her Majesty's pleasure for some time and then you will be turned over to the International Criminal Court for your crimes against humanity." replied Bat.

"I'm not who you think I am." she screamed at them.

Suddenly Ben was struck with an epiphany. The creature in the cell before them bore a very strong resemblance to the cyclist that knocked him about on the Keswick to Penrith rail line walking trail. Could it be that it had been the enigmatic warlord Miss Teak that had dispatched Picov Andropov? It made sense. He would prepare a statement for Logan in the morning.

"You can't hold me. If it hadn't been for that incompetent lorry driver you never would have caught me. Don't walk away from me. Do you hear? You can't keep me here." the enraged villain shrieked at their backs.

The three men turned and walked from the cells out into the fresh air. Bat turned to Ben and pondered, "I wonder what made her run off the road?

What was she on about diamonds melting and a lorry driver? I wonder what she did with the diamonds. There was no lorry nor any other vehicle. She was the only car on that road. She had a significant lead on us and might have escaped."

Logan put in, "How...? I mean where...? Have you...?"

Ben looked at his friends with a sly smile and a conspiratorial wink, "An Illusionist never reveals his secrets, my friends. However, Logan, if you look in the evidence locker in a file box labelled 'Miss Teak' you'll find what you are seeking.

Where will you go now this is over, Bat?"

"I have much work to do. The R.O.M.T. remains a threat so I'm off to Sierra Leone first thing in the morning.

And you? Will you resume your vacation?"

"No. I think vacations are too stressful. I need to get back to work to unwind."

"If you're looking for work the International Criminal Court would benefit immensely from your extraordinarily unique skill set, wealth of specialized knowledge, and your powerful and eminently elite, highly confidential catalogue of personal contacts. The President of the ICC has asked me to extend his personal invitation to you to attend a meeting in the Hague. They put a helicopter at your disposal should you choose to accept."

"I'll need a day or two to think about it, Bat."

Ben had a big decision to make. If he had come away from this holiday with anything it was that he had a lot of work to do alone but he was having way too much fun doing it. He had been on the brink of burn out when this all started. Perhaps he needed an apprentice.

He couldn't stop thinking that all those souls who lost their lives and all those lives ruined could have all been saved if someone could have interceded all those years ago. They had no one to save them from the calamities visited upon them by the evil in life. They had no Avenger or Deliverer.

24 CAT AND THE COP

Logan had slept soundly and awoke refreshed and eager to spend some quality time with Lady Christine. The air was fresh and clean. The sky clear blue and cloudless. He had a spring in his step and a song in his heart as he drove the winding road from the village of Toadspool in the Dell through Monks Wood to Monks Hall.

Pulling to a stop at the door step of the Countess Vera Lee Isay Monk's apartment and stepping from the Vogue Cat came running to greet him. Although she was very pleased to see him there was something else on her mind. "I'm so glad to see you, Logan."

"Just a few loose ends to tidy up and I hope we can begin where we left off." he said with a hopeful smile.

"I'm worried about Chip. He's been acting strange." Logan gave her a look. "I mean stranger than usual. I haven't seen him since last night and he didn't come down for breakfast. His car is still in the garage. I checked. I've looked everywhere for him."

Taking his phone out of his pocket he called Sergeant B. Goodman to enlist his help and asked him to bring Jarvis. The pair arrived within a few

152

minutes and Logan said to the butler, "The Viscount has gone missing, Jarvis."

"How can I help, sir?"

" Do you have any idea where he might have gone?" he asked the butler hopefully.

"You say you've check in all of the rooms, M' Lady?" the butler addressed Lady Christine.

There are one or two rooms that might have been missed, sir."

"Can you show us these rooms, Jarvis?"

"Right this way, sir."

Following on the butler's heels Jarvis led them into the Countess' library. "Whenever His Grace, Viscount Charles, would go missing as a lad this is where he would be found." Reaching out his hand, Jarvis pulled on a first edition of Rudyard Kipling's 1894 classic, The Jungle Book pulling it towards himself as if to remove it from the shelf and to everyone's astonishment a click of a latch releasing was heard and a section of the book case began to move and there inside was the Viscount curled up on the very dusty floor unconscious. He had been sick and his breathing was very laboured.

"Oh, thank heavens and thank you, Jarvis." cried Lady Christine as she raced to his side raising his head and telling him everything was going to be alright.

"From the symptoms he's displaying I'd guess he's been poisoned." ventured the DCI.

Logan told the Sergeant to radio for an ambulance immediately. Chip's left eye was almost closed and had changed a lovely shade of blue and green.

"Who would have done this, Logan?" demanded Lady Christine.

"It was a nightmare. There must have been ten of the blaggards or maybe fifteen. I tried to fight them off but there were just too many." Chip mumbled as if in a dream.

"Oh, you big girl's blouse there was only one assailant and she was a tiny little wisp of a thing." scolded his Grandmother who had followed them. Then turning on Logan she asked crossly, " And what took you so long young man?"

The Viscount seemed to stir to lucidness "What did she want?" asked Logan.

"I'm sure I don't know." whinged the Viscount.

"Of course you do, Charles. She kept asking you where the rest of the diamonds were." corrected his Grandmother.

"Yes, well... She did bring a bottle of my favourite champagne, Dom Perignon White Gold to celebrate. I couldn't resist just one glass.

She asked me about missing diamonds and I tried to tell her I didn't know what she was on about but she wasn't having any of it. Then she waved a pistol at me she would shoot me and Grandmamma if I didn't tell her where they were. So I said she might find what she wanted in my bedroom hidden in my sock drawer under a false bottom for safe keeping, you understand. I told her she might find one or two missing for expenses for looking after them.

I begged her not to shoot me but she just laughed. That's when she hit me with a sucker punch knocking me for six. I must have hidden in here when she went to look for the diamonds."

Cat gave him a look of derision saying, "And left your poor defenceless Grandmamma out here alone. You are a pitiful specimen." as turned on her heel helping her Aunt back to her room.

"But I was so frightened." he whined and promptly passed out.

It was then the paramedics arrived bundling the Viscount onto a gurney for immediate transport to the hospital.

Lady Christine had settled her Aunt into her bed for a nap and went in search of Nurse Barb Bituwitz RN to make certain that she rested. All Cat found in the nurse's quarters was a uniform. The nurse had vanished. She summoned the Countess' Lady's Maid, Tina Crumpet to sit with her. Quietly closing the door to her Aunt's rooms she found Logan and told him of her suspicion that the maid and Miss Teak were one and the same.

"That makes sense. So that's why your brother has been watching the house."

Linking her arm through Logan's asking, "Can you imagine that spineless jellyfish running away to hide leaving Aunt Vera to fend for herself?"

"It's all over now. The courts will decide how to punish him.

Now, where were we before this all started? Oh, yes. We were enjoying a nice picnic by tranquil waters, just the two of us. I had the publican's wife prepare a special hamper for us."

"It sounds like a wonderful idea."

Later, that afternoon, they gazed out over a shimmering lake watching tiny wavelets wafted by a gentle breeze breaking on the beach pebbles glistening in the sunshine. After a sumptuous repast the contented couple lay languorously on a blanket, the warm rays of the afternoon sun making them lethargic. Sheltered from public display by the silent company of a stately old oak tree they shared a tender kiss.

22332029R00089

Made in the USA
Columbia, SC
28 July 2018